(As dictated to my secretary, Bony)

Let's just get a couple of things straight. I was very disappointed to see that the first volume of my adventures was called 'Avril Crump and her Amazing Clones'. Everyone knows it ought to have been entitled 'Augustus the Dog and his Extraordinary Exploits'. After all, it was I who helped my clone companions, Eddy and Bonaparte, escape from Leviticus Laboratories after we popped up in an accidental explosion. It was I who starred in a school play, escaped the clutches of a fiendish clone sent to kill me, and I who foiled my evil creator, Professor Gideon Blut, in a heroic attack that shall be sung about for generations. And what was Avril Crump doing while I achieved these miracles? Running about the countryside like a headless chicken trying to me, that's what. And she got the book named after her. So, for all my devoted fans, here is the second volume of what should rightly be known as 'The Augustus Sagas'.

I declare my story open.

AVRIL CRUMP

and the slumber code

Also by Angela Woolfe

AVRIL
CRUMP
...and Her
Amazing Clones

APRIL CRUMP

and the slumber code

(Part Two of 'The Augustus Sagas')

Angela Woolfe

EGMONT

It was I, Augustus the Dog, who selected Angela Woolfe to set down these events. She was once a student of History, and thus has some understanding of my great imperial ancestry.

Angela lives in London, a city I one day intend to rule, or where at the very least I shall light up the West End stage with my talents. This is her second novel – and not, if I keep giving her such good material, her last.

As dictated to my ~~loyal servant~~ ~~greatest~~ ~~admirer~~ ~~official poet~~ secretary,
Bonaparte

EGMONT

We bring stories to life

Published in Great Britain 2005
by Egmont UK Limited
239 Kensington High Street, London W8 6SA

Text copyright © 2005 Angela Woolfe
Cover and illustrations copyright © 2005 Oliver Burston

The moral rights of the author and illustrator have been asserted

ISBN 1 4052 1893 2

1 3 5 7 9 10 8 6 4 2

A CIP catalogue record for this title is available from the British Library

Typeset by Avon DataSet Ltd, Bidford on Avon
Printed and bound in Great Britain by the CPI Group

Contents

Prologue

One Month Earlier

There was something going on in Room 237.

As darkness fell, four men, their bulky frames wrapped up against the biting east wind, made their way through Gargoyle Woods to the low bunker in the small clearing. They reached the bunker's steel door and the hook-nosed man at the front raised a hand and knocked three times. The door opened.

A dark haired woman stood before them, slender and elegant in tight black clothing and high-heeled shoes. Her face was almost completely obscured behind large sunglasses, and her lips did not smile a welcome.

'He's been expecting you.'

High heels tapping on the bare floorboards, the

woman led the men across the room to another door on the far side. This was labelled in small print: Room 237.

'Room 237?' The hook-nosed man raised a hairy eyebrow. 'Where's the other two hundred and thirty six rooms, then?'

'Yeah.' Another of the men spoke, taking off his woollen hat to reveal a shaven head on top of his heavily tattooed neck. His nose, just as large as his colleague's hooked one, was flattened out across his brutish face, as though he had once been hit very hard with a heavy frying-pan. 'We was told we'd be working for the owner of Gargoyle Manor.'

The dark-haired woman raised a thin smile. 'I see you don't read the newspapers. Gargoyle Manor burnt down three nights ago. It appears that it was set alight deliberately by the clones he was experimenting on there.'

She pressed down on the door handle, then paused for a moment.

'A word of warning,' she said. 'Do not react to his face. Your job is simply to help us get the Replication Chamber from Leviticus Laboratories so that he can return his looks to their former glory.' She pushed the handle again, and the door opened.

'Go on. Don't keep him waiting.'

'Welcome!' A voice rang out from the darkness of Room 237. It had a rasping tone, as though its owner were in pain, but despite this it was still commanding. 'Won't you come on in?'

The four burly men exchanged glances, and then, one by one, they stepped into the darkness. The door was closed behind them.

There was a figure in the very centre of the room. No one could see his face. 'Forgive this darkness,' he rasped again, 'but I do not wish anyone to see me . . . in this condition.'

'Was it the fire at Gargoyle Manor?' asked the hook-nosed man.

The shadowed figure took a step closer. He stretched out a hand and grasped the man by the wrist, causing him to flinch. His hand was scaly and flaking, like a reptile shedding its skin. His face remained shrouded in the darkness. 'Do not mention the Manor,' he hissed. 'I do not wish to be reminded that my Great Work has gone up in smoke . . .'

'Yes, boss . . . Sorry, boss,' gasped the hook-nosed man, unable to loosen his strong wrist from the serpentine grip.

'Besides, it was not the fire that injured me.' The figure suddenly seemed to suffer a spasm of pain. 'Only one person . . .' he managed to gasp, 'is responsible for this tragedy. *Avril Crump.*' He let go and retreated again. 'She inflicted these wounds on me with an exploding doughnut. And when I have mended myself, *I will wipe her out.* I want you to get me the Replication Chamber. My associate will give you your instructions. That is all for now.'

He tapped a foot sharply on the floor, a signal for the door to be opened again. A pool of light came in through the open door, lighting up the shadowed figure. For a moment, his face was visible. The four men looked at him in horror until he pulled back into the dark, covering the charred flesh with shaking hands.

'Get them out, Sedukta! *Get them out!*'

The men needed no more urging, and stumbled from the room.

'Replication Chamber?' said the hook-nosed man, when he was sure the door was tightly closed. 'He's gonna need a lot more than a Replication Chamber to fix *that* face.'

'Yeah,' agreed his tattooed colleague, picking idly

at his frying-pan-flattened nose. 'He's gotta work on the *inside*, too. That's what all the magazines say. We're only as beautiful as we *feel* we are.'

Now that he was alone, Gideon Blut began to rock back and forth. He was singing to himself, two words over and over. It was a name. 'Avril Crump . . .' he murmured. The pain of his wounds seemed to worsen at the very sound of her name, but he could not stop himself from saying it. 'Avril Crump . . . You thought you had defeated me, Avril Crump . . . But you didn't, Avril Crump . . . *And you never will . . .*'

1

The Experiment

It was midnight, and Wretchford-on-the-Reeke was fast asleep.

Inside the garage at Number 56 Icarus Street, a solitary Bunsen burner glowed orange through the darkness. It lit up rickety wooden shelves piled high with tightly-capped jam-jars, labelled in large, uneven felt-tip handwriting: MAGNESIUM SULPHATE – NOT FOR NIBBLING, and SULPHURIC ACID – DO NOT MISTAKE FOR FIZZY LEMONADE. An assortment of Petri dishes and test-tubes vied for space with the scores of large bowls and glass beakers that littered the shelves. Inside the beakers, illuminated by the Bunsen flame, were various mixtures, all brown in colour. Some were so thick that metal spatulas were standing upright in them; others were weak and watery. Piles of old papers and documents lined the walls, most loose in stacks, others spilling out of a cardboard box labelled LEVITICUS STUFF: SORT OUT OR CHUCK OUT.

There was a large workbench in the centre of the garage. Suspended above this was a row of pulley ropes hanging down from the ceiling. On the top of the workbench, directly beneath the ropes, was a large box, about a metre deep and almost as high and wide. This box was constructed out of six supersize take-away pizza containers, coated in a special silver paint that made them flame-resistant. Beside the silver box lay a metal tray, deeply indented in several places, one indentation filled with the special mixture.

Everything was ready for the experiment.

As the flame flickered, three distinct shadows were cast up on the bare concrete wall. One was very short and round. A second was extremely tall and thin, with a large three-cornered hat on its head, while the third shadow appeared to have four legs and a long tail, but perhaps that was just a trick of the light. Suddenly the short, round shadow spoke.

'This is it, chaps,' said Avril Crump. Her hand

reached out and opened a wide flap on the silver-painted box to reveal the heat and light of four more Bunsen flames inside. Carefully, with a tea-towel wrapped around her hand, she checked the position of the metal grille that was wedged in securely just above the four flames. 'Great things could happen in this lab tonight.'

'It's not a *lab*,' said Augustus the dog, proprietor of the peculiar shadow with the tail. 'It's a *garage*. And a pretty damp and uncomfortable garage it is, too. Can't we just get on with it?'

'But I prepared a speech!' Avril reached into her lab coat pocket and drew out a scrap of paper. 'Peanut Butter,' she declared, squinting at it in the soft Bunsen light. 'Raspberry Ripple Ice-cream and Chocolate Biscuits.'

'A wondrous speech!' declared Bonaparte, the tall, hat-wearing shadow, clasping thin hands in rapture.

'Absolutely wondrous, for yesterday's shopping list,' snorted Augustus. 'The Roman Emperors – my great ancestors, by the way – would never have hailed the huddled proletarian masses on the steps of those old amphi-whatsits with yesterday's shopping list.'

'But Augustus, you're *not* descended from the

Roman Emperors! I've told you all the people I think you were cloned from . . .'

There was an icy silence.

'Er, look, shall we just forget about the speech?' Avril said hastily, her boom-and-squeak voice high-pitched with tension. 'It's not really my style anyway. I just wanted to say that this is a great moment in the history of experimenting, a leap for scientific progress and, most importantly of all, a jolly good wheeze all round. Therefore, I declare this experiment . . .' Avril reached for the metal tray on the workbench, placing it on top of the grille inside the silver box, '. . . open!'

She shut the flap. Three pairs of eyes focussed on the closed silver box.

'If it's going to work . . .' whispered Avril, 'it will happen any minute now . . .'

Nobody breathed. Nobody even moved. Then, from inside the box, there came a low sound.

It was a sizzle.

'Did you hear that? How did that sound to you? And what about the smell?'

A warm, sweet aroma was filling the air.

'It's working.' Avril could not take in the enormity

of what was happening. 'After all this time – I think we've cracked it.'

A bell suddenly rang. It came from a large red alarm-clock on the workbench.

'They're ready!' Avril gasped. 'That clock's been customised to the nearest millisecond – more or less . . .' She reached for the gas tap to switch off the flames inside the box, then pulled a rather large and ugly bronze fob watch from her pocket and flipped it open. 'Now the cooling! I'll time it. Action stations, Bony!'

Bonaparte let out a delighted shriek and reached for one of the long strings hanging above the box. With a mechanical whirring, the top of the silver box opened up, at the same time as a large pair of bellows descended from the ceiling. The bellows puffed out until they were filled with air, then exhaled automatically. Expanding and contracting every three seconds, they blew clouds of cooling air into the box until Avril snapped the old fob watch shut.

'Twenty-nine point four seconds exactly. They're cool.'

She reached inside, gently prised something from the metal tray, crossed her fingers tightly, raised it to her lips, and took a first, quick, scientific nibble.

Then a second, gargantuan, horse-like bite.

'It worked!' Avril sank to the floor like a tennis champion. 'We've done it! The Perfect Chocolate Muffin!'

The muffin was a beautiful shade of dark brown, the still warm chocolate chips melting into the sponge. It had a crisp, crunchy outer crust, and a hint of chewiness within. It was not too rich; it was not too sweet; it had neither too few chunky chocolate chips nor too many.

'Praise be!' cried Bonaparte, throwing his hat in the air.

'Before we get carried away,' said Augustus, 'I think *I* ought to taste it. Some lights, Bonaparte, if you please. I'd like to check it's not green or purple or something before I eat it.'

The electric lights went up, making them blink and rub their eyes behind thick protective goggles. Avril staggered to her feet, tripping over two enormous ceramic bowls of muffin mixture, and switched off the flickering Bunsen on the workbench. Bonaparte, dressed beneath his three-cornered hat in a smart red uniform complete with medals and a lilac frilly apron, delicately took the remaining half-muffin from her hand and bore it ceremoniously towards the large, mud-coloured dog, who now spoke again.

'Thank you, Bony,' said Augustus. 'Be ready to take notes, please.'

'At thy service, Mr Dog!' Bonaparte seized a piece of paper from the top of the LEVITICUS STUFF box and produced a stubby pencil from his apron pocket. 'I humbly await thy expert assessment.'

The dog chewed at the half-muffin on the floor, then raised a paw.

'Take this down,' he said.

'Speak forth, dear Mr Dog! I eagerly await thy erudite paragraphs, so brilliantly expressed, so expertly analysed . . .'

'Tasty,' said the dog. 'Really . . . rather . . . tasty.'

'Oh, Mr Dog!' Bonaparte scrabbled to write it down. 'What finesse!'

'Don't forget the *rather*,' said the dog. 'That's very important.'

Avril had found her voice again. 'Do you honestly think we've cracked it, Augustus? All those days, all those nights, all that *mixture* . . .'

'My expert testimony stands,' Augustus said,

already trotting to the garage door. 'Really rather tasty. Now, knock up the rest of the batch, will you, Crumpy? I'm going to get Eddy to make me a drink while I wait.'

'Right you are!' Avril was already reaching for the bowl of mixture on the workbench and turning the heat on again inside the silver box. 'Bony, a piece of paper, if you please! We need to write this muffin formula down.'

'Indeed, Lady Avril!' Bonaparte handed her another sheet from the LEVITICUS STUFF box. 'Was not Mr Dog's a superb analysis?' He peered at the notes he had just written on his own piece of paper. 'Oh!' he said. 'There are some other scribblings here already.'

'Probably just some of my old Oil Spill Sponge designs,' said Avril. 'I used to do them in the Leviticus staffroom at teatime when no one would talk to me. I tell you, Bony, resigning from that horrible laboratory was the best decision of my life – that and bringing you three home to live with me.'

'I thank thee, Lady Avril, but 'tis not a sponge design. And behold – tis another hand entirely.' He suddenly gasped with excitement. 'I may be but a simple scribe and stew-maker, but it doth look like a scientific formula to my ill-educated eyes.'

Behind the words 'Really rather tasty' in Bonaparte's flowing handwriting was another, unfamiliar hand in green ink : *If accidental activation occurs, Slumber Code will trigger. Maximum time limit = 40 days. GB*.' Avril could make out neat, precise numbers and letters too. 'This looks like a formula, Bony, but if it's from Leviticus, I can guarantee it won't be as interesting as my Perfect Chocolate Muffin Formula. You could mix that up from any old things I've got on these shelves.'

'Thou hast the ingredients for this mysterious potion?' Bonaparte's eyes were wide and glassy with desire. 'Might I be permitted to tinker with it, dear Lady Avril? I would so love to impress dear Mr Dog with such alchemy.'

Avril could not help but smile at the clone's enthusiasm. It reminded her of her own first encounters with experimenting. 'All right, Bony. Tell me what the letters and numbers say and I'll give you what you need.'

As Bonaparte happily weighed out the powders that were given to him, Avril busied herself with the next batch of muffins. She placed three large dollops of mixture into the indentations on the metal sheet, one for each of her friends. It was a shame that Eddy had not been there for the moment of great discovery. Avril could hardly wait to tell her.

'Perfect Muffin . . .' she scribbled down the precious muffin formula on the waiting piece of paper, 'is three parts flour, one part butter, two parts sugar and two parts milk, one part egg . . . and five point four parts chocolate chips . . . cooked for eight point five three minutes at two hundred and eighty-two degrees.' Avril sighed with pleasure and held out the formula to admire: $PM = [3F+B+2S+2M+E+5.4cc] \times 8.53m @ 282$. Just then, Augustus came running back in.

'While you two idle about mixing things, *I* have discovered something important.' The dog's brown eyes were fixed on Avril. 'Look, I'd like to break this to you gently, but I'm afraid I can't. It's Eddy.' He took a deep breath and sat back on his hind paws to make his announcement. 'She's gone.'

2

Eddy's Left Hand

'*Gone?*' Avril stared at the dog as though he had suddenly started speaking Latin.

'Yes, gone. Out like a light; dead to the world; on her forty-first wink; away,' Augustus twitched an ear, 'with the fairies.'

'You mean she's asleep?'

'Isn't that what I said?'

'*Again?*' Avril gave up reaching for the bellows cord. She picked up the hot tray of muffins with the corner of her lab coat, took them out of the box and put them on the workbench to cool. 'But she's been asleep almost all day! Most of yesterday as well . . .'

'Alack!' Bonaparte had got hold of a box of matches, eager to start up another Bunsen burner for his own experiment, but had forgotten to blow the struck match out and, more importantly, to drop it. Avril spun around just as the flames rose from the already-flaming piece of paper and up his sleeve. She grabbed a tea-towel from the stack on the floor and flung it over his arm in time to stop the fire spreading.

'Oh, 'tis a most dangerous business, this alchemy.' Bonaparte stared at his singed sleeve. 'And my poor formula, burned to a crisp!'

Crisis over, Avril turned back to the dog. 'Where is she? I'm going to see if she's all right.'

'On the sofa,' Augustus called after Avril as she hurried out of the garage and towards her front door. 'Come on, Bony,' he said over his shoulder, trotting after Avril at some speed. 'We can help wake her up.'

'Edna?' Avril hurried through the scratched, red front door. 'Edna, you must wake up! I've got wonderful news about the muffins . . .'

Eddy was lying beneath a tartan blanket on the threadbare green sofa, her soft brown hair fanned out on the armrest. The little girl's face was half covered by an old blue pullover that had belonged to Avril when she was about the same age as Eddy was now. It was at least three sizes too large and rode up around her chin. Above the dark blue wool, Eddy's green-and-amber eyes were closed. Her skin was a waxy shade of grey. She was not moving.

Avril gasped and fell to her knees beside the sofa. 'Get me a mirror!'

'*Now* you decide to take an interest in your personal appearance?' Augustus stared at her. 'It may be long overdue, but is it really necessary at a time like this?'

'To see if she's breathing!' Avril was racking her brains to remember what the doctors and nurses in TV hospital dramas did. She picked up Eddy's limp hand and tried to feel for a pulse in the wrist, but she knew from the time she had accidentally blown up her geography teacher's packed lunch that pulses were tricky things to find. Poor Mr Mulally had been halfway to the morgue before a faint pulse (and pulverised pieces of prawn sandwich) had been detected just behind his ear. 'Bony, please stop wailing,' she begged, as the tall clone set about renting his lilac apron and tearing at his straggly hair. 'She's not dead, she's just asleep . . . isn't she . . .?'

Augustus bounded back into the room with a hand mirror between his teeth. 'Here.' He dropped it beside Avril, who picked it up and held it beneath Eddy's nostrils.

'So apart from the scenic view up Eddy's nose, what exactly are we looking for?' Augustus asked, just as Avril let out a yelp of joy.

'She's all right! She *is* breathing – look!'

Sure enough, a faint patch of condensation had gathered beneath Eddy's nostrils on the mirror.

'Oh, happy day!' Bonaparte performed a little jig. 'The Fates do smile upon us – our dear Miss Eddy is alive and well!'

'I don't know about *well*.' Augustus was studying the limp, grey figure on the sofa with his head on one side. 'She looks like she's gone through the washing machine.'

'She doesn't look very good,' Avril agreed, feeling a little bubble of fear rising in her stomach. What would she do if Eddy really *was* ill? She remembered cool baths and spoonfuls of revolting medicine from her childhood, but that had always been a result of overdosing on cake. She had no idea what to do with someone who would not wake up.

'She *never* looks very good.' Now that the danger to Eddy's life was averted, Augustus was examining himself contentedly in the hand mirror. 'Always frowning and scowling about something.'

Avril stared at Augustus in surprise. 'She always looks cheerful to me.'

'That's because she's friendly to you. Says you need moral support or something. Says you're still upset about those clones who died in the fire at Gargoyle Manor. Why she doesn't think *I* might need moral support, I don't know. It's not an easy life, being adored by millions.'

'Thou hast *my* support, Mr Dog!'

Augustus waved a regal paw in acknowledgement.

'Edna said that?' wondered Avril. 'But . . . well, I'm quite all right . . . I hardly think about the fire . . . perfectly fine . . . just getting on with my muffin experiments all day, every day . . . *Oh*.' Her shoulders drooped. 'I've been neglecting you, haven't I?'

Augustus, never one to let an opportunity pass him by, pricked up his floppy ears. 'Yes,' he said sadly. 'It's been very upsetting for *all* of us. Cooped up here with nowhere to go and nothing to do . . .'

'Thou hast thy hectic schedule of TV quizzes and soap operas, Mr Dog!'

Augustus glared at Bonaparte before adding a sniff

for Avril's benefit. 'It's not the same,' he sighed, 'as *freedom*. Eddy keeps talking about going to school, you know. It breaks my heart,' – another sniff – 'to see her suffer so.'

Avril covered Eddy with the tartan blanket and got to her feet. Her forehead was creased deep. 'She did *mention* school. But it's just so dangerous. If anyone found out who – *what* she was . . .'

She picked up Eddy's hand again and gave it a squeeze, but still she did not stir. It was then that something on Eddy's hand caught Avril's eye. She peered closer. 'There's something really weird going on here . . .'

'Oh, don't sweat it, Crumpy.' Augustus hopped up on to an armchair and stretched out. 'There's nothing to worry about really. Eddy's just lazy. She's *always* dozing off here, there and everywhere. In the bath, in front of the TV . . .'

Bonaparte nodded in agreement. 'On Saturday e'en she did fall into a slumber while I gave my recitation of my latest ode, *Mr Dog, The Brave and Bountiful Bottom-Biter of Gargoyle Woods*.'

'Look, we've discussed this before,' began Augustus, the hairs on his neck standing on end. 'I

21

don't *want* my epic sagas to be filled with other people's posteriors!'

'Has either of you written something on Edna's hand?' Avril suddenly asked. Her face was a little more pink than usual as she stared at Eddy's hand, holding it up to the light for a better view.

'No indeed,' said Bonaparte. 'I know for certain that I have not done such a thing, and Mr Dog is unable to write.'

'Not *unable*,' snapped Augustus. '*Unwilling*, Bony, *unwilling*.'

'But there's . . . a *number* written on her hand. Look.' Avril thrust the sleeping girl's left hand towards the others, who came forward to inspect it. There, on the back of Eddy's hand, was a large, two-digit number.

18

'Eighteen,' said Bonaparte, in puzzlement. 'What meaning has this, Lady Avril?'

'I don't know.' Avril could not tear her eyes off the number. Now that she was looking at it more closely, it did not look like it was written *on* Eddy's hand at all, but underneath the skin instead, in a blue-green colour. 'Maybe it's a tattoo. But when would she have got a tattoo? And why the number eighteen..?'

Then, as the three of them stared at the mysterious number, something even more peculiar happened. Smoothly, surely, like a digital clock-face changing its display, the number eighteen under Eddy's skin became a number seventeen.

'*Seventeen*!' gasped Bonaparte, taking a leap backwards. 'What dark magick is this, Lady Avril?'

Avril's eyes met Augustus', as wide and bewildered as her own. 'I have no idea . . .' She blinked very hard and shook her head, but when she opened her eyes and stared down at Eddy's hand again, the changed number was still there.

17

The doorbell suddenly rang.

'Augustus. You haven't ordered pizza *again*?' said Avril.

'No!' Augustus bristled. 'Do you think I'm some kind of addict or something?'

'But nobody ever rings the doorbell apart from the pizza people. And it's almost one o'clock in the morning!'

'Well, maybe we're such good customers that they've decided to deliver us a *surprise* pizza.' Augustus' tail gave a sudden, involuntary wag and he bounded to look out of the window. 'Oh,' he said, turning away in disinterest. 'It's just *him*.'

A mousy-haired boy was standing on the doorstep, shivering with the cold, and pushing his glasses up his nose nervously. His duffle coat was not thick enough for the freezing winter night, and his mittenless hands were curled into helpless protective balls.

''Tis Young Master Wilfred! Perhaps his dread father, Dr Nasty, has allowed him to visit us after all.' Bonaparte's face split into a huge beam as he hurried to open the front door.

'Bony? That w-was quick! I d-didn't think anyone w-would be awake,' came Wilfred's voice. 'The bell didn't d-disturb anyone, d-did it?'

'Fear not, Young Master Wilfred! Only Miss Eddy doth slumber.' Bonaparte was already pulling the boy into the living room. 'Allow me to introduce my dear friend, Lady Avril.'

'Wilfred! How nice to meet you. This is a surprise. But you've come at a rather difficult time . . .'

But Wilfred was opening his mouth at the same time. The two of them spoke in unison.

'I think there's something terribly wrong with Eddy.'

3

Emails

From: Wilfred
WetherbyJunior@WetherbyMail.com
To: Eddy
Eddy85@ChezCrump.com
Subject: Hi

Dear Eddy

How are things? I wish you could come back to school, but maybe Avril will change her mind soon. Keep working on her. Then we'll both have someone to talk to all day.

My dad only 'remembered' to give me the letter you sent this morning. He's always up earlier than me to do his clarinet practice, so he gets to the postman

25

before I do. Still, I suppose I should be grateful he gave me the letter at all. He usually doesn't in case they're from Mum. Anyway, hope this is the right email address – it was a bit difficult to read your letter with all the stew stains, so let me know if this gets to you all right.

I got picked second from last for the class cricket match on Friday, so that was better than usual. Dad's letting me tinker with his old moped engine in return for me working harder on my Geography project. He let me stay up late to watch a documentary on Ice Age beetles the other night, even though I really wanted to get a DVD from the shop. We made hot chocolate with mini marshmallows. Things are OK.

Wish Dad would let me come round and see you. I think he's still spooked about the fire at Gargoyle Manor. I hear him shouting about it in his sleep sometimes, but he never mentions it.

How's Augustus and the others? Wish I'd seen him talking!

Yours truly

Wilfred

From: Eddy
Eddy85@ChezCrump.com
To: Wilfred
WetherbyJunior@WetherbyMail.com
Subject: Re: Hi

Wilfred! it was so great to get your email thank you Avril has been showing me how to work email and the internet I really think im getting the hang of it

glad to hear about the cricket things are ok here too though Avril working on the muffin all the time it distracts her from thinking about the fire at the manor I know she feels bad that she could not save any of those poor clones. She never mentions it either She is very busy i have tried to tell her I would be fine at school and no one would realize i am a clone. Lets face it no one would even talk to me! I told her that but she just looked sad so i haven't asked again. Avril needs us more than ever now that she has no job and is sad about the fire. we have to be careful we are not found out.

am sometimes a bit bored. i fall asleep most

afternoons. maybe soon (fingers crossed) avril will not worry and I can go to school and will not be so bored. And you will have someone to talk to!

Miss you email back love Eddy xxx

From: Wilfred
WetherbyJunior@WetherbyMail.com
To: Eddy
Eddy85@ChezCrump.com
Subject: Re: Hi

Dear Eddy
Sorry to hear you are bored. If I could I would come to visit but Dad would throw such a wobbly if he found out. He made me spend five hours on the Geography project at the weekend – he's thought up a New Improved way to do graphs and wanted me to learn all about it. My project will probably get 100% and then everyone will spit in my packed lunch again.

Yours truly, Wilfred

From: Eddy
Eddy85@ChezCrump.com
To: Wilfred
WetherbyJunior@WetherbyMail.com
Subject: Re: Hi

Hi Wilfred sorry only just got the email have been asleep all afternoon and even missed supper it was a special cauliflower stew bony had made and he was upset so now I have to eat it cold and say how delicious Sorry to hear about project and hope no spitting will email more tomorrow am very tired so will go to bed right after stew miss you love eddy xxxxx

From: Wilfred
WetherbyJunior@WetherbyMail.com
To: Eddy
Eddy85@ChezCrump.com
Subject: Re: Hi

Dear Eddy

You won't believe it but I got 17% on my Geography project! The lowest mark ever given, Miss Dougall said. Am a bit of a hero at school now – even got to sit on a table with some of my class at lunch today. Wish you had seen that. It was dad's New Improved graphs that did it – Miss Dougall said she's never seen such a load of old rubbish. Dad's been on the phone to the headmistress and the school governors all evening. He says either Miss Dougall resigns or he'll stop St Swithin's from going to his new Science for Kids Week at Leviticus. He's cross with me as well and he's taken the moped engine away. Write back soon, Eddy – I want to know what you think!

   Yours truly
   Wilfred

From: Wilfred
WetherbyJunior@WetherbyMail.com
To: Eddy
Eddy85@ChezCrump.com
Subject: Re: Hi

Dear Eddy
Are you all right? You didn't reply to my email
yesterday. Is everything OK?

Yours truly
Wilfred

From: Eddy
Eddy85@ChezCrump.com
To: Wilfred
WetherbyJunior@WetherbyMail.com
Subject: Re: Hi
Wilfred im so sorry I was so tired yesterday I slept all
day from after breakfast til nearly ten o'clock and
then forgot to check the computer I think I must be
getting a cold or something because im so sleepy but
have no runny nose so perhaps not!!! I love all your

news from school I told the others all about the geography project Avril thinks your dad is being unfair and augustus says he always knew miss dougall was a sensible woman at heart I hope you have got the engine back I have to go now as Bony is giving a recitation and last night I slept right through it will be in big trouble with Augustus if i miss it again. Is almost like being at school, at least that is what I think! Email back, please Wilfred. I can't wait to hear more about miss dougall. love eddy xxxx

From: Wilfred
WetherbyJunior@WetherbyMail.com
To: Eddy
Eddy85@ChezCrump.com
Subject: Re: Hi

Dear Eddy
You seem to be sleeping a lot. It sounds like you sleep for longer and longer every day. Is everything all right?
    Yours truly
    Wilfred

From: Wilfred
WetherbyJunior@WetherbyMail.com
To: Eddy
Eddy85@ChezCrump.com
Subject: Re: Hi

Eddy – no reply – are you sleeping again?

From: Wilfred
WetherbyJunior@WetherbyMail.com
To: Eddy
Eddy85@ChezCrump.com
Subject: Re: Hi
Eddy, I'm serious. You haven't replied since the day before yesterday. I think something must be wrong. Maybe I could phone you. What's Avril's telephone number? I'll have to do it late or Dad will hear me. Try to be awake at eleven pm.

From: Eddy
Eddy85@ChezCrump.com
To: Wilfred
WetherbyJunior@WetherbyMail.com
Subject: Re: Hi

Oh Wilfred am so sorry again I slept right past eleven pm and didn't even wake up til lunchtime it has been a strange couple of days avril is very close to getting her muffin formulation right and bony and augustus have been helping I wanted to help but cant seem to stay awake long enough You mustn't worry Wilfred there is nothing wrong it is probably just too much stew or the cold or something I am sure I will not sleep so much all the time any news on the engine? Love your best friend eddyxxx

4

The Slumber Code

It was like floating in a lake, with the sun shining down gently. It was like dipping your knife into a jar of the most fragrant honey, and spreading it thickly on hot, crisp toast. It was like dancing to the sweetest music, finding that your limbs could do anything you wanted them to. There was no one in this place to make you feel awkward or unwanted. Voices welcomed you, begging you to join. In musical tones, they sang out all around, until through the heavenly noise there came a discordant, almost painful sound; another voice.

'Battle of the Somme.'

She did not want to leave yet; she did not want to go back to a place that was cold and sometimes lonely.

'Battle of the Somme, you moron!' An irritable

sigh. 'You don't deserve to be on a quiz show! *Battle of the Somme*!'

Sunlight . . . dimming . . . voices . . . fading . . .

'Time's up,' bellowed an announcer's voice from the TV screen. 'And the answer is – the English Civil War.'

Eddy opened her eyes from the deepest of deep sleeps to see the back of Augustus' head above her. He was watching the TV screen, his front paws hovering over her own head.

'Like I said, the English Civil War. What sort of idiot doesn't even know *that*?'

'Augustus?' Eddy's limbs ached after so long spent lying on the lumpy green sofa. 'Augustus, what's going on?'

'You're awake!' Augustus turned round to face her, his eyes widening in surprise. 'I knew it! I *can* heal with the power of touch.' He prodded her on the nose with a rather sharp claw.

'Ow! What did you do that for?'

'I have used my Extraordinary Powers of Healing to bring you back to consciousness,' Augustus announced. 'You can't lie around looking dead all day and expect me to do nothing.' He prodded her again, but less hard this time. 'I shall use this power for good, Eddy,' he said solemnly. 'I have been given the Gift.'

Eddy stared at the dog's face as he set about jabbing her in various locations. His usual expression of satisfaction had been replaced with something rather different, and he would not look her in the eye.

'Gus, what's wrong? Where is everyone?'

When he set his ears back and refused to answer, she sighed and tried again.

'All right, all right. *Augustus*. Where is everyone?'

'Oh, around and about.' Augustus said, holding her down rather firmly with one front paw on her stomach while circling the other mysteriously about her head. 'Lie still, Eddy, for the laying-on of paws . . .' He closed his eyes and inhaled deeply, then began to hum, rather off-key.

'*Death!*' Suddenly there came a terrible howl from the direction of the kitchen. 'Death, death, and murderous maladies!'

Augustus stopped humming. The only movement was the tip of his tail, which flicked nervously.

'*What* did Bony just say?' Eddy stared at Augustus.

'Alas and alack for poor Miss Eddy! A tragic life –

so sweet and yet . . .' – Bonaparte's voice convulsed into sobs as stew-pans clattered – '. . . so dreadfully short . . .'

Eddy's green-and-amber eyes widened and she struggled to sit up. 'What's he talking about, Augustus? What's going on?'

'Look,' Augustus said, pressing his paw more firmly on her stomach, 'I can't possibly work my magic if you're constantly writhing about like a python.'

'Augustus, let me get up. I won't be kept in the dark like this.' Eddy flung off his paw with some effort and got to her feet. Black dots danced about her eyes as she adjusted to being vertical for the first time in hours, and she steadied herself with one hand on the back of the sofa. As the dots began to clear, she could see the steadying hand more clearly. There was something written on it, in what looked like blue-green ink.

15

'Augustus, what have you done to my hand?'

The dog's whole body tensed. 'Nothing!' he said. 'Anyway, Eddy, let's not talk about that. When *you* can heal the sick with the merest touch, then we might find time to chat about your hands. Right now,' he yawned ostentatiously, 'I'm afraid you're being a tad tedious.'

'But someone's written the number fifteen on my hand!' Eddy said. 'Why?'

'*Fifteen?*' Augustus gulped. 'It can't be! I healed you only two minutes ago! You're ruining all my hard work.' He pushed her back on to the sofa. 'And concentrate this time.'

'Augustus, let me go!' Eddy raised her voice above his humming and managed to get to her feet. 'I'm going to find Avril. I want to know what's going on.'

Augustus darted about her feet, trying to trip her up as she made for the door.

'If you just stayed still and let me lay my paws on you, Eddy, we'd solve this little problem in a jiffy.' He blocked her way to the door to the hallway. 'Who are you going to trust? Crumpy and stupid old Wilfred, or the Miraculous Augustus, Hero of . . .'

'*Wilfred's* here?' Eddy got around Augustus and opened the door. 'At *this* time of night? Where is he?'

There were voices coming from behind the closed dining-room door, and the blue glow of a computer coming from underneath it.

'. . . but what are we going to do?' Avril's voice came from behind the closed door. It was high-pitched and tense, very different from her usual warm tones. 'We're not going to find anything on the Internet about *this*!'

'W-we have to try, Avril,' came Wilfred's voice. 'What other choice do we have? Professor Blut's the one who caused the problem and he's the only one who could cure her. But he's d-dead!'

At that moment, Eddy tripped over Augustus' carefully-placed tail and almost fell over. She steadied herself on the nearby banisters just in time to hear Wilfred's voice again.

'Maybe my d-dad could help. I know you two don't see eye-to-eye, but I'll ask him if you w-want me to.'

'That's very kind, Wilfred, but your dad knows no more about genetics than I do. Whatever Gideon did to Edna's DNA, it's far too complicated for an ordinary scientist to solve.' There was a loud sniff. 'I have to do *something*, and fast! I couldn't save any of those clones from the fire, but I'm not going to let Edna go. If we don't find a cure, she'll be dead by six o'clock tonight.'

In a mad rush, Augustus ran at Eddy's feet and she tumbled on to her hands and knees on the wooden floor with a loud clatter. She saw the dining room door fly open through swimming eyes. The two faces that stared down at her were white with fear. Eddy looked up at Wilfred, all the joy of seeing her friend for the first time in weeks stuck beneath a heavy weight in her heart. 'Wilfred? How did you get here?'

Like Augustus, Wilfred could not look Eddy in the eye. He pushed his glasses up his nose with a trembling hand.

'I sneaked out while D-dad was doing his aerobics DVD in the spare room. He puts it on when he can't sleep, which is most of the time these days. I waited until he was on Beautiful Buns and Tighter Tums to be sure he w-wouldn't notice me going.'

'You walked across Wretchford by yourself?' Eddy let Avril pull her to her feet. 'But it's so dark, Wilfred. And so cold out there.'

'I had to see you right away, Eddy. The moment I worked out there was a problem . . .'

Avril stopped Wilfred by laying a hand on his arm. 'You mustn't worry, Edna. We're going to find you a cure.'

'A cure for *what*? Why won't anyone tell me? And why have I got this number written on my hand?'

41

Wilfred pushed his glasses up his nose and stared at Eddy. 'It was in your emails, Eddy,' he said. 'You've been sleeping more and more each day – winding down, like an old mechanical clock.'

'So I've slept a lot.' Eddy was trying to remain calm. 'So what?'

'Eddy, there's never been a human clone before. Nobody knows how they work, what kind of defects they might have . . .'

'*What kind of defects they might have?*' Eddy could hardly say the words. She looked away from Wilfred's gaze. 'I'm *me*, Wilfred. I'm not some kind of test-case.'

Avril spoke. 'But we don't think the problem is simply because you're a human clone, Edna. We think something extraordinary is happening. Something Gideon did.' She took Eddy's hand and stared at the number. 'Fifteen,' she murmured. 'So it's still going down . . .'

'What does it mean?'

Avril took a deep breath. 'Bony found this piece of paper in my old Leviticus junk.' She passed it to Eddy.

'*If accidental activation occurs,*' Eddy read, '*Slumber Code will trigger. Maximum time limit = 40 days. GB.* I don't understand. What's the Slumber Code?'

'Today is forty days since the explosion in Lab One,' Avril said. 'That's when you were accidentally activated. GB are Gideon Blut's initials. He must have added this Slumber Code, whatever it is, to your DNA when he first mixed it all up all those years ago.'

'So once my forty days are up, I'll fall asleep forever . . .?' Eddy stared down at her hand, where the number fifteen seemed to be growing more vibrant in colour. 'This number. It's counting me down from midnight. You said I'll be . . . dead by six o'clock this evening.'

'No,' Wilfred said, helplessly. 'W-we're not going to let that happen.'

'But I heard you. You said you couldn't find anything to help!'

Avril gazed at Eddy. 'Only Gideon knew what he did to your DNA.' Her shoulders sagged. 'And I killed him.'

There was silence in the hallway for a moment. Eddy felt sick. She stared at her two best friends, seeing defeat in their eyes.

'Please,' she said. 'Please help me.'

Suddenly, Avril's shoulders snapped up again. A thought had just struck her like a speeding fire-engine.

'Gideon,' she said. 'That's it. We need Gideon.'

Wilfred spoke before Eddy could. 'But Avril, he's d-dead.'

'Yes, yes . . .' Avril ran a hand across her bald head, something she only did when she was thinking very hard indeed. 'Gideon *is* dead. But his technology isn't. The thing that *created* you isn't . . . Not completely . . .'

Eddy stared at Avril. She suddenly knew exactly what she was about to say.

'*The Replication Chamber.*'

★

Wilfred scribbled down his father's entry code for Leviticus, then stared around the garage as Avril threw things into a large black rucksack. 'W-why doesn't my d-dad have anything like this in our garage?' He wandered over to a side table cluttered with bowls and pushed his glasses up his nose. 'Gosh. What a lot of muffin mixture.'

'Thanks for the entry code, Wilf.' Avril put it into her rucksack with a torch, a balaclava, and a length of thick rope. 'Now, will you promise me you'll stay and look after Edna until I'm back from Leviticus with the

Chamber? I need to know she'll be all right.'

'But Avril, my d-dad doesn't even know I've sneaked . . .' Wilfred stopped, and gulped in a fortifying mouthful of air. He pushed his glasses up his nose again. 'Yes,' he said. 'Of course I'll stay. D-dad can stuff it. It's an emergency, after all.'

'Thank you, Wilf. I wish I had a friend like you.' As Avril shrugged the rucksack on to her back, one of the large black straps caught on the beaker of colourless liquid that Bonaparte had concocted earlier. The beaker tipped sideways and the liquid spilled all over the workbench, oozing towards the second batch of Perfect Muffins.

'Bother Bony and his alchemy!' Avril snatched the tray up, but not before the smallest muffin was saturated in the liquid, soaking through its white paper case. It seemed to drink it up like a sponge, and was dry almost immediately.

'That's w-weird.' Wilfred stared at the small muffin. 'What was that liquid?'

'Oh, it's harmless stuff. Just Bony messing about.' Avril picked up the small muffin and popped it into her rucksack, then emptied the rest of the muffin tray into the bag too. 'Emergency snack rations,' she told

Wilfred solemnly. 'It's very bad luck to go on a mission without them. And heaven knows, we need more luck now than we've ever needed before. Now, you're *sure* you remember your dad saying the Chamber was still in Lab One?'

Wilfred nodded. 'He said so only two weeks ago. He was complaining about the mess you'd left behind in Lab One when you resigned.'

'Right. I'll be there and back by six a.m., speed limit or no speed limit.' Avril flung a floor-length coat on over her lab coat. 'We'll have twelve hours. Then we can really get to work.'

Wilfred gulped. 'Do you really think the Chamber can cure her?'

'It's Gideon's cloning technology.' Avril was already on her way out of the garage and towards the cherry-red front door. 'That's where he messed up her DNA to start with, and that's what we're going to use to save her.' She gave Wilfred a grim thumbs-up before opening the front door. 'I've done some wild experiments before. We'll crack this, Wilfred. And Gideon's Chamber will help us do it.'

'Right.' Wilfred returned the thumbs-up with nervy defiance.

Avril set her face into a bright beam and hurried into the living room, where Eddy and the others were waiting to see her off. 'Off to Leviticus in the dead of night – this is an adventure!'

Nobody beamed back. Bonaparte sniffed and mopped his eyes with the edge of his lilac apron. Augustus hovered a paw over Avril's feet and closed his eyes.

'I'm channelling my powers into you,' he intoned. 'I shall be with you in spirit, Crumpy.'

Avril suddenly fumbled in her pocket, brought something out and went to Eddy. 'Take this,' she said, pressing the ugly bronze fob watch into the little girl's right hand. 'It was a gift from poor old Uncle Edgar. I customised it years ago, so it'll tell you the time to the nearest tenth of a second. You see?' She flipped open the heavy, battered lid. 'It's almost four o'clock now. I'll be back before two hours are out. You keep an eye on that watch-face, Edna, and remember I'll be back in no time at all.'

'Oh, Avril.' Eddy squeezed her hand. 'Thank you very much. I'll take good care of it.'

'Oh, it's nothing!' Avril blinked several times, rather rapidly. 'It's a bit of a lucky charm for me.

Brought me luck in every experiment I ever did. Apart from the ones where innocent by-standers were injured, of course . . .'

This time, Eddy managed a smile.

'But Lady Avril, is't not a terribly dangerous mission?' Bonaparte's voice wobbled.

Avril waved a hand. 'Not in the least. No one will even know I'm there. All the night-time security guards at Leviticus were laid off months ago. It was the same cutbacks that got rid of chocolate biscuits in the staffroom at tea-time. Shocking, shocking . . . Anyway!' She shook herself. 'You four stick together. If I'm not back by six o'clock, call Lionel and tell him what's going on. He'll think of something.'

'Call Lionel,' said Eddy. 'Got it. But – Avril, you will be all right, won't you?'

'Of course I will!' Avril gave them a salute and hurried away. The cherry-red door slammed shut behind her as she got into her little green sports car and started the engine.

'Fourteen hours and counting.' She put her foot down hard on the accelerator, and roared off down the road towards Leviticus.

5

Early-Morning
Ramblers Anonymous

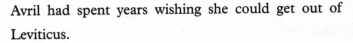

Avril had spent years wishing she could get out of Leviticus.

Now she would have given her last doughnut to get in.

Dr Wetherby's entry code was not working. Rucksack on her back, a thick layer of camouflage mud smeared over her face, Avril stood outside the electronic gates in the early-morning darkness, a hundred metres from the looming, rounded Victorian tower on the west side of the old brick building. Lab One, and the Replication Chamber, would be at the top of that tower. Avril was ready for the mission. She had keyed in the five-number sequence at least ten times now, but the gates stubbornly refused to budge.

Wilfred must have made a mistake, she thought desperately, as she tried the sequence one last time. Nine-one-three-six-seven. Still nothing. Instead of the click and whirr of the electronic mechanism, she could hear something else.

Not very far away, a dog was barking. Then, as Avril held her breath, she saw the sweep of a torch and heard the purr of an engine. Accompanying the dog was a security guard, prowling the perimeter on a motorbike.

'But . . . there *aren't* any security guards these days . . .'

Nevertheless, Avril could not deny that a security guard was exactly what was coming towards her, and she had absolutely no desire to become an angry Alsatian's late-night snack. The barking was getting closer, and now she could see it would only be a few seconds before the dog picked up her scent, a heady mixture of muffin mixture and damp earth. Hands shaking, Avril keyed in the code again, crossed her fingers, and said a little prayer to the patron saint of electronic keypads.

But the gate remained closed.

The motorbike headlight suddenly dazzled her. Heart pounding, camouflage mud beginning to run in little rivulets down her sweating forehead, Avril stood her ground.

'Jolly old morning for a ramble,' she said loudly and, she hoped, heartily. 'Tell me, am I far from Crinkled Bottom?'

'Get on the ground!' yelled the guard above the barking of the dog, who was straining at the leash that held him on the back of the motorbike seat, and looking at Avril very much as she might look at a plate of French Fancies. 'Now!'

'That's not very polite.' Avril took a careful step backwards. 'I certainly won't be sharing my special Ramblers' Flapjacks with *you*.'

'Funny sort of time for a ramble.'

'Oh, but this is the very best time! Nothing like a lovely long early-morning ramble to get the blood pumping. There are hundreds of us, you know. Early-Morning Ramblers Anonymous.'

'Where?' Avril could hear the fear in the guard's rough voice as he swung his headlights suspiciously into the surrounding foliage. 'Come on out, the lot of you!'

'No, no – not *here*. Just – you know – *around*. Rambling. Up hill and – er – down dale. All that sort of thing.'

Now that the lights were not shining into her eyes, Avril could see the guard's face. He had a flattened nose that looked as if it had been hit with a frying pan, and several colourful tattoos. He was at least twice her height and built like a barrel. There was a touch of the Auntie Primula about him. He did not look like any of the regular guards Avril could remember from her days at Leviticus, and he was not wearing their regulation navy-blue uniform.

'This is private property,' he said, pulling at his dog's leash. 'Shouldn't be rambling here. Main road's half a mile that way.'

'Oh, what a shame.' Avril's voice boomed out uncontrolled. 'It isn't at all the same, rambling on a main road. Really takes out that all-important ramble factor. Are you sure you won't just tell me the way to Crinkled Bottom?'

'Now you listen to me . . .' Suddenly the radio on the guard's massive shoulder buzzed.

'*Watervole to Rattlesnake, Watervole to Rattlesnake. Come in, Rattlesnake.*'

'Shouldn't you answer that?' Avril was desperate for the distraction.

The guard blinked at her. 'I'm not Rattlesnake!'

'Well, shouldn't you answer anyway? Watervole doesn't sound very happy.'

The guard picked up the radio. 'Red Herring to Watervole. Red Herring to Watervole.'

'*You're not Red Herring, you idiot. You're Rattlesnake.*'

'I thought I was Red Herring.'

'*You're not Red Herring.*' A different voice suddenly whined out of the radio. '*I'm Red Herring.*'

'Since when?'

'*Mother Mary told me I could be Red Herring. I've always wanted to be Red Herring. I would've been Red Herring right from the start if you hadn't pinched it.*'

'Hey! That's not fair . . .'

Avril started to creep away, fixing her eyes on the Alsatian's, willing him not to bark at her. All these red herrings were working to her advantage.

The first voice came back on. '*This is Watervole again. Look, Rattlesnake, will you just get back in here? Mother Mary wants all of us up in the West Tower. Lab 99. Now.*'

Avril stopped. Lab 99 was on the eleventh floor of the West Tower, only one flight of stairs away from Lab One.

'I'm not coming,' the guard said tearfully, 'unless I can be Red Herring.'

'*Be like that, then, Rattlesnake. But if you're not up here in five minutes, I'm reporting you to Mother Mary. And she'll report you to Professor Doppel. And you know what happened to the last person who got reported to Professor Doppel.*'

'I thought it was *you* who got reported, Watervole.'

'*No! That was Warthog.*'

'Well, that's just stupid,' reasoned the guard. 'What's the point of us all having codenames if they get confused like that?'

There was a defeated silence from the other end of the radio.

'*That* told him,' said the guard, putting away his radio with an air of triumph.

'What's going on in Lab 99? Who's Professor Doppel?' As soon as she had spoken, Avril was kicking herself for being so stupid. But the guard did not seem to question why a Rambler would possibly want to know about late-night activities at Leviticus.

'It's a Secret Mission,' the guard said, importantly. 'The boss – that's Professor Doppel – wanted us to get this Chamber for him. That was a few weeks ago. Now he's working here, see, and we're looking for something else . . . hang on.' The guard frowned. 'It's s'posed to be a Secret Mission. I better not say no more.'

The Chamber? Somebody else had the Chamber? 'No! Tell me more! I mean . . .'

Then a new voice crackled out from the guard's radio. This time, it was a female voice, barely audible with its low purring tone. As it spoke, the already freezing air temperature seemed to drop by several degrees.

'Rattlesnake, this is Mother Mary speaking. You have five minutes exactly, Rattlesnake. I will not be kept waiting.'

The Alsatian on the back of the bike let out a little whimper, which Avril almost echoed. Even through the weakness of the radio frequency, the voice was chilling. And familiar.

'Yes, Mother Mary. Right you are, Mother Mary.' The guard sounded as terrified as the dog looked. Completely forgetting about the stray rambler with her strange questions, the guard switched his engine on and set off towards the back gates at some speed.

Avril was not sure if this was very good luck or rather bad. The guard had left her alone, taking his psychopathic pet with him, but she was still no closer to getting into Leviticus. And now she knew that somebody else had the Replication Chamber. This

Professor Doppel, with his strange private security guards and Secret Missions, was an unexpected and unwanted obstacle.

'But I need that Chamber . . .'

Avril began jogging wheezily around the entire circumference of the perimeter fence towards the entrance the guard had just used, hoping against hope that he had left it open. But it was hopeless. The back gates were locked as tightly as the front, and Dr Wetherby's code did not work there either. Then, suddenly, Avril remembered something.

'I can't believe I've been so stupid!'

All the time she had been trying that entry code had been utterly wasted. There was another way into Leviticus, a sure-fire way that did not need entry codes or open gates of any sort. Avril dropped to her knees and began to feel her way along the damp grass. It had to be here – a raised metal ridge. Her fingers were so cold that she could hardly feel the ends of them, let alone anything on the ground. Then she hit something with her right knee.

Completely covered with grass, it was a square patch about one metre by one metre. Avril got to her feet, reached for the ring handle that she hoped would still be there. It took over ten minutes of heaving until the metal lid came loose. Avril fell backwards, whooping with delight. This was it. This was her way in to Leviticus. The secret tunnel.

6

Old Friends

It had been years since Avril had even thought of the tunnel. During her early days at Leviticus, she had secretly freed the laboratory animals. Avril's daring midnight rescues through the old underground passage had ended forever when the Chief Governor's favourite beagle went AWOL and they had sealed off the animal area to all but high-ranking personnel.

But the tunnel had never been discovered.

Avril dropped herself carefully into the hole, her feet hitting soft muddy ground, before reaching up and out to pull the manhole cover back over the entrance again. It was stinky and dark down beneath the foundations of Leviticus. She clamped a hand firmly over her nose and reached out to guide herself along with the other. The walls were slimy too, thick with moulds so fertile that they glowed green through the darkness. Avril briefly pondered taking a sample for her Fascinating Fungi collection, but decided that the pong was just too offensive.

Slipping slightly in her compost-coated Wellingtons, she lifted her free hand up to the ceiling to thump about for the trapdoor. When she thumped something loose and wobbly, she knew that she had found it. The patch of ceiling here was not made of concrete; she knew this because of all the painful splinters now sticking out of her fist. Avril reached into her pocket for the woolly hat she had brought. It would provide just enough protection from splinters. She pulled the hat over her smooth head, braced herself for impact, and began to batter herself against the trapdoor.

Suddenly, somewhere through the reverberations in her head, Avril heard a voice from above.

'No! *No!* There is nothing to steal in here.' The voice was shaking. 'I advise you to stop battering your way in and leave immediately. I should also warn you,' it continued, 'that use of that tunnel contravenes seven separate regulations in the Leviticus Code of

Conduct. Not to mention basic health and safety provisions, which you have utterly disregarded with a shamelessness bordering on . . .'

'Raymond!' Suddenly recognising the voice as Dr Wetherby's, Avril banged her head quite accidentally against the trapdoor in amazement.

There was a gasp. 'How do you know my name? You're not a burglar at all, are you? You're a Creature of the Underworld!' There was a loud thud as Dr Wetherby flung himself against the trapdoor. 'Begone with thee, foul demon of Hades! I've done nothing to deserve this, nothing! I've never lied, never cheated, I'm kind to dumb animals . . .'

Avril snorted.

'All right, all right, so you know about Hamish the Hamster! But I was five years old, damn it. I don't deserve to go to hell.'

'Raymond, please just help me out . . .'

But Dr Wetherby had begun a Latin incantation, and was not listening.

'Raymond, it's me, Avril Crump!'

Dr Wetherby let out a moan before he managed to speak. 'It is *I*.'

'Well, I know it's you, Raymond.'

'I *meant*,' – Dr Wetherby's frown was almost audible through the floorboards – 'that it is grammatically incorrect to say, "It's me." The proper phrase is "It is I."'

There was a thud of heavy footsteps as he got to his feet, then a creak of a hinge as he pulled the trapdoor open and peered down into it.

Avril flung open her arms, her boom-and-squeak voice reverberating through her chest. 'Raymond Wetherby, I could just hug you!'

'That won't be necessary.' Dr Wetherby, who was wearing a pristine white polyester tracksuit and brand new trainers with the label still on, took several hasty paces backwards as Avril clambered out of the tunnel. 'You smell horrendous.'

'I know. Sorry about that. We'll save the hugging until after I freshen up a bit, shall we?'

'Or, alternatively, until hell freezes over.'

'Oh yes, hell.' Avril grinned at him as she brushed the larger clumps of stinking fungi off her clothing. 'Not a big fan of hell, are you, Raymond? Foul demons of Hades and all that.'

Dr Wetherby scowled. 'I'd rather not talk about that, thank you.'

'Oh, Raymond, just the same as ever! It's so wonderful to see you.' Avril could not help but beam at him. 'I haven't seen you since . . . well . . . since that night . . . in the woods . . .' The words stuck in her throat, and Dr Wetherby looked away. The fire at Gargoyle Manor had been traumatic for both of them.

'So, Dr Crump,' he said loudly, 'perhaps you might like to explain to me *exactly* what you think you are doing, breaking into my office at this ungodly hour on a Saturday morning.'

'*Your office?* But I thought this was one of the Animal Storage Labs.' Avril looked about. Although the room was only dimly lit, she could see several dozen cages lining the walls, and there was a good deal of high-pitched squeaking.

'Yes, well . . .' Dr Wetherby strode to a small, rickety desk in the corner and rifled through a pile of files, authoritatively. 'I've moved out of my old office for a while to conduct some important research in here. My study into the bonding of intermetallic powders and inert carbon to refine crude oil is reaching its most fascinating stage yet!' He was turning magenta. 'Besides, this lab is the headquarters of my new Christmas Science for Kids initiative.

Yuletide experiments, Santa Claus giving out enjoyable science-themed goodies, unemployed actors wandering about dressed as festive lab rats. You know the sort of thing.'

'What a wonderful idea! But Raymond . . .'

'Anyway, this is all beside the point. You resigned over a month ago, Dr Crump. What on earth are you doing back here?'

'You have to help me, Raymond. It's Edna.'

'Ha!' Dr Wetherby snapped a file shut. '*That* little madam. She's turning my Wilfred against me, with seditious letters and insidious emails! Already his schoolwork is slipping.'

'Oh, but Wilf's a hero, Raymond. He's the one who realised there was a problem with Edna. He's at Chez Crump now, in case you were worried about him. He's perfectly safe.'

'Wilf . . . I mean, Wilfred, is *where*?' thundered Dr Wetherby. 'I thought he was tucked up in bed, possibly reading a thrilling mathematics textbook under the covers by torchlight, but nothing as insubordinate as *running away* . . .'

'Oh, but he didn't run away. He just wanted to tell us the bad news about Edna.'

'Bad news?'

'There's a . . . malfunction, Raymond. With Edna.' Avril took a shaky breath. 'Gideon did something to her DNA when he mixed it up years ago. It's called the Slumber Code. He made sure that if she was ever brought to life, she'd only last a maximum of forty days. Today's the fortieth day, Raymond. We've only got . . .' – she stared up at the clock on the wall – 'twelve and a half hours left.'

Dr Wetherby frowned. 'That sounds bad.'

'But I'm going to stop it, Raymond!' Avril clenched a fist, and winced as the splinters dug in. 'I'm going to find a cure.'

'A cure?' Dr Wetherby smirked. 'Dr Crump, your greatest scientific quest to date has been to create an outsized mop for oil spills. The best geneticists in the world do not understand how human cloning works.'

'It wasn't a mop, Raymond,' Avril sighed. 'It was a sponge. Now, are you going to stand about being sarcastic, or are you actually going to help me?'

'How could I help you? *If* I agreed to do so.'

'You can help me steal the Replication Chamber.'

Dr Wetherby let out a low moan. 'I do wish you wouldn't use words like *steal* . . .'

'Then we'll work out how to use it to re-program Eddy's DNA! There's only one problem.'

'*Only one?*'

'Somebody else is using the Chamber. A Professor Doppel, to be precise.'

'Doppel?' repeated Dr Wetherby. 'I know the name. Not met him, though. He only arrived from Scandinavia a couple of weeks ago. What could he possibly want with a burnt Replication Chamber?'

'Who knows? But he's got lots of Security Guards up in the West Tower. And that's exactly where we have to go to get that Chamber.'

'Guards?' Dr Wetherby had turned pale.

'But that doesn't frighten us, does it, Raymond?' Avril squared her shoulders and headed for the door. 'We've got to save Edna, and no violent guard or snarling Alsatian is going to stop us!'

'Hang on – I didn't say I was going to help.'

'I know, Raymond,' Avril said over her shoulder as she hurried down the dark corridor. 'You didn't *say* you were going to help.'

But his footsteps were already resounding behind her.

7

Supersize Ham and Pineapple

Eddy awoke with a jolt. The wonderful, warm haze of sleep was gone in an instant, as soon as she came back to consciousness. There was a distinct ticking noise echoing in her ears, which she quickly realised was just the old battered heater rattling away in the corner. All the lights were out, and it was dark outside on Icarus Street. There was nobody else in the room.

'Everyone?' Eddy was suddenly afraid to be alone, and she did not dare look down at her left hand. 'Guys, where are you?'

'In yon kitchen, Miss Eddy!' came Bonaparte's voice. 'Art thou awake?'

Eddy pushed the rickety door from the living room into the kitchen. 'What are you doing? Where's Wilfred?'

Bonaparte looked up from the huge pan he was stirring on the stove. 'Young Master Wilfred hath fallen into a light doze in front of yon computing machine,' he said, waving the wooden spoon towards the dining room for emphasis. 'Thou must forgive me, dear Miss Eddy, for I know that he is your very dear friend, but the poor lad doth appear to be two parsnips short of a hotpot.'

'What do you mean?' The bright light in the kitchen was making Eddy's eyes sting.

'He means,' came Augustus' voice, 'that the kid's not terribly bright.' Eddy peered over to where the dog's voice had come from: behind the open lid of a pizza box on the kitchen table. He was wearing Wilfred's glasses and working his way methodically through a supersize ham and pineapple pizza with extra olives. 'He doesn't seem to realise just what an extraordinary being I am. I told him to order me a pizza, and he made an extremely foolish remark about a *dog biscuit* topping.'

'He is but a poor cretinous soul,' sighed Bonaparte.

'I'm sure Wilfred didn't mean anything,' said Eddy. 'He just thinks you might like dog biscuits.'

'Then he is not only an imbecile, but a heretic,' said Augustus.

'I hope you didn't scare Wilfred.' Eddy glared at the dog. 'He's not used to seeing a talking dog, let alone an extremely bossy one.'

Augustus was silent, which Eddy attributed to a rare moment of shame, but was in fact because a large chunk of pineapple had just gone down the wrong way.

'Miss Eddy! I know that thou art tragically afflicted with a dreadful genetic curse and have but a few hours to live, but there is no call to be slandering dear, honourable Mr Dog! Why, if Lady Avril had returned from her daring late-night dash, I do believe she would be ashamed of thee!'

'*Avril's not back?*' Eddy scrabbled in her pocket for the fob watch, feeling it cool and heavy in her hand as she flipped the lid open. There were two tarnished and horribly elaborate gold-leaf hour- and minute-hands on the original decorated watch-face, and a bright red plastic second-hand whirling around a separate, newer dial in the middle. This newer dial was marked out in tiny gradations of a tenth of a second, and ran so fast that it made Eddy's eyes hurt.

She stared at the old gold hands instead. 'But . . . it's gone half past six in the morning. She swore she'd be back before six.'

Unwillingly, but unstoppably, her eyes crept down to look at her left hand for the first time since she had woken.

12

'Has she phoned?' Eddy put the watch back into her pocket with shaking hands.

'No,' said Augustus. 'And the phone's been free *all the time*, hasn't it, Bony?'

'Indeed, Mr Dog. Apart from thy repeated telephone calls to yon pizza delivery man, of course.'

Augustus glared at Bonaparte. 'That was meant to be a secret!'

'Forgive me, Mr Dog! But there are so many secrets I must keep. Why, only last week I did keep thy secret about the terribly unfortunate effect my cauliflower stew had upon thy sensitive aristocratic digestive system . . .'

'That cauliflower was undercooked, and you know it!'

'You shouldn't have used the phone to order pizza!' Eddy could feel the panic rising. Avril had been gone for nearly three hours, with not so much as a whisper.

Augustus jumped off his chair and sat in front of a high pile of pizza boxes behind him, so that Eddy could not see how many there were. 'I only had one or two,' he told her smoothly. 'There was a special offer.'

Bonaparte waved a pepperpot. 'I do believe it was an "Order Five Supersize Ham and Pineapple with Extra Olives, Get Nine Free" offer, was it not, Mr Dog?'

Augustus let out a guilty burp.

'Eddy? I thought I heard you. I'm sorry I w-went to sleep . . .' His hair sticking out at a series of improbable angles, Wilfred staggered into the kitchen. He was groping blindly without his glasses and addressed the cooker. 'Eddy, is Avril back?'

'No,' Eddy said shortly, reaching for the telephone on the wall. 'I'm going to call Lionel. He'll know what to do. Augustus, give Wilfred back his glasses. He can't see a thing without them,' she added as she dialled the number.

'But they make me look so terribly distinguished.' Augustus admired his reflection in a metal spoon.

'Lionel?' Eddy spoke into the receiver as it was picked up at the other end. 'Lionel, it's me. Eddy. We need your . . .'

'Help . . .'

'Well, yes, that's it exactly!' Eddy was relieved. 'We do need your . . .'

'*Help* . . .'

And the line went dead.

Eddy stared at the receiver, then at the three others. 'Did Lionel just yell *help*?'

'Twice,' said Augustus, twitching an ear to remind everyone of his super-powered hearing. Wilfred's glasses, perched precariously, wobbled for an instant and then fell to the floor. 'Whoops.'

'Augustus!' Eddy snatched the glasses up and handed them to Wilfred. 'You drop Wilfred's glasses and all you can say is *whoops*?'

'*If* you'd let me finish.' Augustus drew himself up and glared at Eddy. 'I was *about* to add "a-daisy".'

'It's OK, Eddy,' Wilfred said hastily, sensing Eddy's temper rising. 'It was just an accident.'

Augustus waved a magnanimous paw.

'I'll call Lionel again. Perhaps it was a crossed line.' Eddy turned back to the phone, her hands shaking as she dialled the number. 'Lionel? Are you there?' she asked as the receiver was picked up.

But there was no reply. There were simply

thudding noises dimly in the background.

'Gus, come here. Listen to this.' Eddy thrust the receiver at Augustus' ears. 'What's going on?'

'Ah. So *now* you allow yourself to acknowledge my greatness . . .' Augustus sauntered to the phone and listened. His expression changed. 'Voices,' he said. 'I can hear voices.'

'Mr Dog can hear voices!' Bonaparte waved his arms at Wilfred. 'Thy heresy has sent him doo-lally!'

'Voices *down the phone*,' snapped Augustus. He looked at Eddy. 'There's someone there. It sounds like they're smashing things up. I can't hear Lionel . . . And now the line's gone dead.'

Wilfred put his glasses back on and peered at Eddy. 'W-what shall we do?'

'We must go there.' Eddy was already running into the living room to find her shoes. 'If something's happening to Lionel, we have to help him.' Her heart was racing and she was on full alert, pushing to the very back of her mind the fervent wish that she had not woken up at all. 'Wilfred, come with me. Bony and Augustus, you stay here.'

'Hey! That's not fair. I haven't been out of this cooped-up old dump for weeks!' Augustus caught the look in Eddy's eye and rapidly fashioned a stronger case. 'What I meant to say,' he continued smoothly, 'was that you'll be needing my super-powered hearing again. Won't you?'

Eddy thought about this as she watched a white-faced Wilfred struggling into his duffle coat. 'All right,' she said. 'You can come, Augustus.'

The dog let out a sharp bark of excitement and raced for the stairs. 'Back in a moment!' he yelled, running for the room he shared with Bonaparte.

'Bony, you stay here and wait until we come back,' said Eddy, picking up the tartan blanket. '*Do not go anywhere*. Have you got that?'

Bonaparte nodded breathlessly. 'I shall make a stew for thee upon thy return.'

Eddy hurried out into the hallway just as Augustus came bounding back down the stairs again. He was clutching a large, knobbled stick between his teeth. 'Thought this old stick might be useful protection,' he said, casually, as he placed the stick on the floor with excessive care. 'Found it in the bedroom. Must be Bony's,' he added in a whisper.

Eddy had seen the dog happily wrestling with the exact same stick on several occasions, but she said

nothing. 'Good idea, Augustus,' she said. 'You hang on
to it. It could be our secret weapon.' She wrapped him
in the blanket, for warmth, positioning his stick
between two of the blanket's layers so that it could not
be seen.

Augustus's tail wagged. 'So, we'll grab a pizza,
maybe catch a movie, hit the town . . .' He stopped as
he saw Eddy's glare. 'And rescue Lionel, obviously,'
he muttered, before trotting over to Wilfred and
placing a paw on his knee. 'It's your lucky day, kid.
Despite your earlier forays into shameful heresy, *you*
have been selected as Imperial Canine Bearer Of
The Day.'

'What?' Wilfred blinked nervously at the dog. 'I d-
don't understand . . .'

'You don't *need* to understand.' Augustus hopped
up into Wilfred's arms, making the boy stagger and
gasp with the sudden weight. 'You just need to carry
me.'

'But . . . I can't . . .'

'You can thank me later,' Augustus said
generously, snuggling down in his blanket. 'Right now,
we've got Lionel to save, haven't we, Eddy?'

'Remember, Bony, just stay here.' Eddy held the

door open for Wilfred as he lurched out with Augustus. The tall clone waved at them from the kitchen doorway. 'If Avril gets back, tell her what's happened. We'll be back with Lionel in a few minutes.'

8

Resurrection

The grey-painted corridors of Leviticus Laboratories were very still. There was a low electric hum emanating from beneath most of the closed laboratory doors, but no other sounds disturbed the eerie peace. Avril and Dr Wetherby hurried down the darkened hallway.

'Righty-ho,' Avril whispered, as they reached the end of the corridor and pushed open the doorway that led into the West Tower. 'When we get to the eleventh floor, just keep going up the last flight of stairs as fast as you can. Hopefully no one will come out of Lab 99 and see us.'

Dr Wetherby rolled his eyes but gave a nod.

'I'll lead the way!' Avril mouthed.

She was scooting up flight after flight on the spiral

staircase, when suddenly she heard something. She stopped, held her breath and listened again.

'Raymond! Stop!' Avril seized Dr Wetherby's tracksuited arm. 'Did you hear a noise?'

Dr Wetherby frowned. 'Well, all I can hear is your horrible wheezing.'

'No, not that. *That.*'

The faint noise that Avril had heard was growing louder. It was like the tapping of a light hammer against a nail, and it was coming slowly but surely down the Tower stairwell towards them.

'Footsteps,' whispered Dr Wetherby.

Avril thought very fast. She pulled Dr Wetherby up on to the nearest landing, and back into the shadows. 'Stay very still,' she mouthed at him. 'Must be those guards again.'

'Rubbish,' Dr Wetherby mouthed back, inexpertly. 'Security guards don't wear high heels.'

Avril was getting a funny feeling in her stomach. Dr Wetherby was right – it *did* sound like high-heeled footsteps. The clack-clack-clack sound against the shiny grey floors was uncomfortably familiar . . .

Suddenly, a radio buzzed.

'Mother Mary speaking,' said the same voice Avril

had heard outside the gates earlier: low and chilling. 'The Chamber? It's been moved to Lab 99 . . . Very well. I'll meet you there in ten minutes.'

Hurrying in shiny black stilettos down the flight of stairs, the woman swung a mane of raven hair, her long fingernails adding accompanying taps to the banisters as she went past.

'I don't believe it,' Avril whispered. '*Sedukta*. I thought Blut had her killed . . .'

'What's *she* doing here?' Dr Wetherby was hopping with indignation, his brand new trainers squeaking on the lino. 'How dare she show her face in these hallowed halls! The woman's a criminal, for heaven's sake. Shouldn't someone have arrested her by now?'

'Raymond, quiet!' Sedukta was not very far away. 'We've got a big problem here.'

'Too right we've got a problem! It's not Professor Doppel. *Sedukta's* got the Chamber!'

'But now we know it's in Lab 99. And she's meeting someone there in ten minutes,' Avril said. 'So we don't have very long.'

She had bounded up three stairs in one leap when she was pulled backwards by the lab coat.

'Are you insane? I'm not going up there now.'

'Raymond, look, I have to get that Chamber home *fast*, or there's no hope for Edna. So I'll nip up to Lab 99 and pinch it, and you stay here and warn me if anyone's coming. Agreed?'

'Hold on!' Dr Wetherby hissed, as Avril sprang in uncharacteristically sprightly fashion up several more steps. 'How shall I warn you? What's the signal? There has to be a signal!'

'Oh . . . hoot like an owl or something,' Avril hissed back.

'Like an *owl*? Well, what species?' Dr Wetherby frowned. 'A Barn Owl sounds very different to a Great Horned . . . Dr Crump? Dr Crump?'

But Avril was already two flights away, and could not hear him. Sedukta's words were ringing in her head: '*I'll meet you there in ten minutes.*' Who was she talking to? Avril pounded up on to the eleventh floor and stood outside Lab 99. She peered through the tiny transparent window in the grey door, squinting from one side of the curved wall to the other as far as her eyes would allow her to catch any glimpse of a Security guard in the room. But there was no one, and nothing, except a large, black leather chair beside the window. Avril pushed the door open and walked into the room.

All the cupboards above the workbench were shut, several even padlocked. Avril picked up one of the wooden stools and began frantically bashing the largest padlock with it. Splinters flew, and one of the stool's legs cracked and tumbled to the floor. The padlock burst and she flung the cupboard door wide, only to see nothing but empty glass beakers. Pulling back her shoulders to set about the next padlock with the shattered stool, Avril heard a footfall outside the lab's door.

She spun around. Dr Wetherby had not hooted! How could he have failed to warn her? She was fully prepared to charge at the opening door with nothing but the wooden stool and a terrible war-cry, and was just filling her lungs for the blood-curdling yell when the door opened wide.

Then all the air was taken out of her, and she staggered backwards into the leather chair. She could not believe who was standing in the doorway.

'Good morning, Dr Crump,' said Gideon Blut. 'What a lovely surprise.'

9

Unwanted Guests

The sign above the door had been torn off its hinges and stamped on. The door itself had been smashed with something heavy, and there was broken glass on the hallway carpet. Eddy could not bring herself to walk into Lionel's sitting-room. She did not know what she would see.

'He's not in here,' said Augustus, who had hopped from Wilfred's arms the moment they had seen what had happened to Lionel's little house, and run into the living room. 'But the place is a mess. Either Lionel's been throwing some wild parties that we haven't been invited to, or somebody came here looking for something. I'll look upstairs.'

Eddy reached for Wilfred's hand as they peered

into the living room. Stuffing had been ripped from the sofa cushions and the coffee table was in pieces on the floor. Every picture on the wall had been torn down, glass smashed and frames ripped open.

'He's not upstairs either,' panted Augustus, running back down. 'Can't smell him anywhere. He's gone, Eddy.'

'Then someone must have taken him.' Eddy picked up a photograph from the floor. Lionel, beaming in his old policeman's uniform, stared back at her. 'Who did this, Lionel?' she whispered. 'Who came here?'

'Now hang on a moment. If there's going to be any psychic deduction, I'm the dog to do it.' Augustus placed his paws over the photo and began humming.

'W-we should call the police,' said Wilfred, sure of himself for the first time. He marched to the telephone and picked it up. 'Oh, no,' he said, as it buzzed uselessly at him. 'The wire's been cut.'

Eddy suddenly shivered. 'I think we should get back to Chez Crump as fast as we can. It's not safe here.'

'But Eddy, Chez Crump may not be safe either.' Wilfred gestured about at the wrecked room. 'This could be something to do with you three, couldn't it?'

'A crazed fan searching for a memento . . .' mused

Augustus. 'A desperate Mr Dog-obsessive beating Lionel to a pulp to get him to reveal my whereabouts . . . All the biggest stars have stalkers these days, you know. I saw it on TV.'

'I don't know what this is,' said Eddy, 'but I don't like it. Let's go.' She pulled Wilfred towards the front door, Augustus bounding behind them. It was still dark, and their ragged breath hung in the freezing early-morning air as they ran along the silent street. 'We can't call the police . . .' She was thinking out loud. 'They'll take us away again, like last time. That's if they even listen to us anyway . . .'

'D-dad.' Wilfred stopped still. 'D-dad can call the police for us. Then you three will be safe. And they'll listen to him. Everyone listens to my d-dad.'

'But Wilfred, then he'll know you've been with us.'

'I'll take the risk.' Wilfred staggered as Augustus leapt up into his arms again. 'My place is only three streets away.'

Nobody spoke as they hurried towards Wilfred's house. Eddy stuffed her frozen hands in her pockets, determined to ignore the number that had now appeared there.

11

She clutched the ugly old fob watch, willing it to bring her the luck that Avril had said it would.

Then there came a shout from Augustus.

'Stop! Everyone, stop!'

Just as they rounded the corner on to Wilfred's street, the dog leapt out of his arms and blocked their way.

'Somebody's here too,' he hissed, jabbing his tail at a white-painted house on the other side. There were two huge black-and-silver motorbikes parked outside on the small driveway.

Wilfred's eyes widened in alarm behind his broken glasses. 'That's *my* house!'

Lights were going on upstairs and down. Large figures, silhouetted against the still-drawn curtains, began lifting and dropping things. There were several loud smashing sounds.

'Dad!' gasped Wilfred, darting towards the house, but Augustus blocked him.

'He's not in there,' the dog said. 'I'd smell him if he were. Particularly pungent odour, your dad. Like Eddy – too much unnecessary soap. But he's not there.'

Wilfred's shoulders sagged with relief.

'You two wait here. I'm going up closer to listen

to them.'

'Be careful, Gus . . . I mean Augustus,' Eddy called after him. Getting down low on his front, he slunk towards the Wetherby's house, ears twitching in anticipation. The voices inside were very clear to him now.

'*You check the drawers again. That's the sort of place a Formula might be, innit?*'

'*How should I know? We don't even know what this Formula's supposed to look like.*'

'*Well, I'm not telling Professor Blut we can't find it.*'

Augustus almost let out a bark of surprise. *Professor Blut?*

'*Shut yer mouth and radio Red Herring. Maybe he's found it at Crump's place by now.*'

Now Augustus did let out a bark. He turned and ran across the road as fast as his four legs would carry him.

'We've got to get back to Chez Crump!'

'Augustus, what's the matter? What did you hear?' Eddy gazed after the dog as he started to run back the way they had just come.

'Don't just stand there asking questions!' Augustus' shout came clearly through the freezing night air. 'Bony's in danger!'

Wilfred pulled Eddy's hand, and the two of them began to run.

10

The Missing Formula

'Gideon . . .' Avril managed to stagger back to her feet. She could not tear her eyes off the figure in front of her. As blond and perfect as ever, there was not even a scratch from the explosion that she had been sure had killed him. He stared at her for a moment, not moving.

'Gideon?' he echoed. A huge guard lumbered in behind him, then closed the door and stood in front of it. 'No. Here at Leviticus I am Professor Doppel, all the way from farthest Scandinavia.'

'*You're* Professor Doppel? But don't they realise . . .?'

'They only know Gideon Blut as the disgraced young scientist who was expelled from here fifteen years ago. Shorter, scrawnier, covered in pock-marks and pustules. How glad I am now that I took all those years to transform my disgusting appearance. Nobody here has recognised me for an instant.' His cold green eyes were fixed upon her, unblinking. 'Well. Avril Crump,' he said. 'I am not sure who is the more surprised.'

'I thought you were dead.' Avril's knees were wobbling and she had turned rather green. 'The explosion . . .'

Gideon's mouth twisted into a ghastly smile. 'The explosion caused me considerable damage,' he said. 'So I had my guards recover the Replication Chamber, which I used to . . . restore myself.'

'You didn't restore yourself – you've *cloned* yourself!'

'I availed myself of the only technology that would save me. *My* technology. But, you see, Dr Crump, there is a problem with the Chamber. When I built it years ago, I made sure that any clones that were created in it would not last for too long.'

'The Slumber Code . . .' Avril breathed.

Gideon blinked, surprised. 'Yes, Dr Crump, the Slumber Code. It is a part of the Replication Chamber's very fabric. I took the risk because I had no alternative. And now . . .' He held up his left hand. There, scarring the soft skin in livid purple, was a number.

11

There was a faint film of sweat on Gideon's upper lip, and his eyes were heavy-lidded. 'Now all I need is the Formula. Which is where you come in.'

Avril blinked. 'What Formula?'

'You know what I am talking about.' Gideon began to stride from one side of the curved lab to the other. 'The only reason I came back to Leviticus was to get that Formula. But we have searched for two weeks, and it is nowhere to be found. You were the last person in Lab One. Until my guards, you were the last to touch that Replication Chamber. I am afraid you are the most likely one to have stolen my Formula. And I must have it, Dr Crump. That Formula is my lifeline.'

'So there *is* a cure for Eddy . . .'

'Eddy?' echoed Gideon. 'The mutant girl?'

'The *perfect* girl,' Avril replied.

'She is *still alive?*'

'Yes.' Avril stared up at him. 'But Augustus and Bonaparte don't seem to be affected.'

'Why not those two?' Gideon hissed, so low that

Avril could barely hear. 'Why didn't the Slumber Code affect *them*?'

'You can't control science, Gideon.' Avril looked up at him. 'That's the real beauty of experimenting. All the things that go wrong. That's when the most exciting breakthroughs happen. It's a shame you've never learned that.'

Gideon was not listening. 'The Code was designed precisely to prevent that sort of filthy, mixed-up mongrel . . .'

'Don't you dare call them names! Who are you to say what's perfect and what's not? And for what it's worth, *I* think Bony and Augustus *are* perfect!'

She fell silent as Gideon turned on her, green eyes blazing. 'Quiet!' he spat. 'You really are the most infuriating, sentimental . . .' He stopped as a sudden, deep yawn stretched his mouth from corner to corner. 'Not a single word more, Dr Crump,' he said, his eyes drooping heavily, and his voice dropping to a whisper. 'I must think. So . . . the girl has lasted the full forty days, whereas I developed the symptoms within thirty-five days. That is an extremely interesting development. What a very special child she must be . . .' He smiled down at Avril, almost pleasantly. 'Unless you hand over the Formula, that special little girl will fall asleep and never wake again.'

'Gideon, I don't even know what this Formula *is*!'

Gideon's ocean-green eyes closed for a split second. 'The Formula makes a serum that infiltrates the damaged DNA to reverse the cell decline that the Slumber Code causes.' He yawned again. 'There is nothing else that will cure us . . .'

Avril's blood was like ice. 'But I *don't have it*.'

'You are lying!' Suddenly, there were shouts from outside the door.

'Take your hands off me at once! Mishandling a senior scientist is against Directives 19 and 20 of the Edict Against the Mishandling of Senior Scientists, 1997!'

'Silence!' Sedukta hissed, opening the door and shoving Dr Wetherby through it, past the silent security guard. 'Professor Doppel, look who was spying on me on the stairs. It is our old friend Dr Wetherfront.' She stared at Avril. '*And* April Crump. All the usual suspects, I see.'

'For the last time, it's Wether*by*!' Dr Wetherby howled. Then he noticed who else was in the room. 'Blut? I don't believe it! You're supposed to be dead . . .'

Gideon got very slowly to his feet. He looked faded now; grey and washed-out. 'Delightful to see you too, Wetherby. Your friend and I have been having a very pleasant chat. Perhaps *you* can persuade her to tell me where the Formula is.'

'Formula? What formula? Dr Crump doesn't even *use* formulas as far as I know. Just makes it all up as she goes along.'

Avril's defeated heart gave a leap. Dr Wetherby had given her an idea. She stared up at Gideon, willing him to fall asleep as his green eyes flickered open and shut like the wings of a dying butterfly.

'One of you will tell me where it is . . .' Gideon was barely audible now, 'or the consequences . . . will be terrible . . .' Almost in slow motion, he turned to Sedukta. 'Get the information I need, Serafina. Come to me in Lab 100 when you have finished.'

'Don't worry, Professor.' Sedukta's voice was thick with pleasure. She drew a syringe from her pocket. 'I'll get it out of them.'

'Dr Crump, if you do not give me the Formula . . .' Gideon was at the door, leaning against it in order to stay upright, 'you will not leave here alive. But if you do hand it over, *I will make some of the serum for your mutant friend.'*

Avril stared at him. She could not trust that Gideon would do anything of the sort, but at that moment, if she had had this Formula, she would have handed it over to him in the blink of an eye.

The guard opened the door.

'Nothing else will cure her.' Gideon drew in a deep, painful breath, keeping his eyes wide open. 'Think about it, Dr Crump,' he said, leaning on the guard for support. 'I am your last hope.'

The door closed behind them.

'So,' Sedukta let go of Dr Wetherby and turned the key in the lock. 'Where shall I begin?'

11

Bony in a Stew

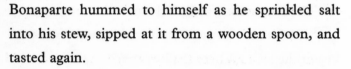

Bonaparte hummed to himself as he sprinkled salt into his stew, sipped at it from a wooden spoon, and tasted again.

'Yet 'tis still a mite insipid,' he sighed, reaching for his enormous pepperpot and preparing to grind. 'How I wish there was somebody here to assist me.'

Then there was a crash as the front door flew open.

'Oh, Mr Dog! Thou hast returned at a most opportune moment!' Bonaparte ran to the hallway, then stopped and stared. It was not Eddy and the others. There were two enormous men standing before him, clad in bikers' leathers. 'Good morrow,' he said uncertainly. 'Art thou friends of Lady Avril?' He peered more closely at the larger of the two men.

'Thou dost bear a striking resemblance to an Auntie Primula that I have seen in several rather disturbing photographs . . .'

'Shut it, bony.'

'Then thou *must* be friends of Lady Avril!' Bonaparte waved his pepperpot in welcome. 'Thou dost know my name!'

'We ain't no friends of no Lady no one,' said the shorter, hook-nosed man. 'Now, you just tell us . . .'

'Aha! I have it now! Thou art surely here to assist me with my stew.' Bonaparte pointed a long finger at the taller man's flattened, mangled nose. 'A terrible frying-pan injury, I see,' he sympathised. 'But it could only be the mark of a great stew-chef!'

'Now, you hold on just one . . .'

'And such charming drawings!' Bonaparte clasped his hands in delight as he gazed at the tattoos on the man's forearm. 'I should also like to display my devotion to my art of stew cookery with such symbols – tell me, is yon illustration of a bloodied meat-cleaver of *particular* sentimental value to thee?'

'Who *is* this clown?' snarled the hook-nosed intruder. 'Deal with him, Rattlesnake.'

'I ain't dealin' with no one,' said the other man,

sulkily, 'unless you calls me Red Herring. And I ain't havin' my nose insulted by no one, neither. Years of therapy to hold me head up high, and then this medieval bozo . . .'

'Just sort him out, will you?' The hook-nosed man was already thudding up the stairs. 'Find out if he knows where it is. And Boss just radioed in new instructions – find the little girl, too.'

'Alas, Miss Eddy is not here at present, and worse, nor is the marvellous Mr Dog. But if thou dost care to wait for their return, I will bring thee a small plate of my humble breakfast stew to taste and . . .' Suddenly the intruder slammed him against the wall with a powerful and tattooed fist. 'Very well!' Bonaparte gasped. 'A *large* plate!'

'Where is it?' snarled Red Herring, breathing hot breath into Bonaparte's face. 'Tell us or you're dead.'

'It? It?' cried Bonaparte. 'I know naught of this It!'

'Talk English!' Red Herring slammed Bonaparte against the wall again, sending plaster showering down. 'And start telling me what I want to hear!'

Bonaparte was close to tears. He could think of only one thing that he was sure the man would like to hear.

'*Mr Dog*,' he announced, '*The Brave and Bountiful Bottom-Biter of Gargoyle Woods*.

The air was chill, the night was dark

When through the trees there came a bark

And there he was – that fearsome fighter:

Mr Dog – The Bottom-Biter . . .'

He paused. 'Perhaps you would care to sit down?' he offered. 'There are another seventy-four thrilling verses to go.'

Red Herring's jaw fell open. 'All we want to know is where the Formula is. And if you don't tell us, you're *dead*, fruitcake.'

'Formula?' Bonaparte's forehead creased. 'Why, I only know of one Formula and that is in Lady Avril's l –'

'Bony!' Suddenly, Augustus rushed in. 'Let him go!' With a snarl, he jumped up and bit Red Herring very hard on the seat of his trousers.

'Oh Mr Dog,' said Bonaparte, as Red Herring let him go, 'how fitting! Thou art just in time for a recitation of *The Brave and Bountiful Bottom-Biter of* . . .'

'Come on!' Eddy and Wilfred were also at the door.

'Miss Eddy, these gentleman have come to visit

us!' Bonaparte turned and called to Red Herring, who was staggering in agony down the hallway. 'Yoo-hoo! Mr Herring! Miss Eddy is home!'

'Bony, they're bad people!' Eddy ran into the hallway just as the hook-nosed man appeared at the top of the stairs. As she pulled Bonaparte towards the door, the man slid down the banisters and grabbed her.

'Bad people?' Bonaparte gasped. Deftly, neatly, he raised his pepperpot and ground several thick sprinkles of black pepper over the intruder's large hooked nose. He sneezed so violently that he let go of Eddy and was thrown backwards against the opposite wall.

Eddy seized the moment. 'Come on!'

Through his streaming eyes, the hook-nosed man could only just see the back of Bonaparte's heels as Eddy pulled him out of the door. He was wiping his eyes for several minutes before he managed to speak.

'This is your fault!' he managed to yell down the hallway at Red Herring, who was moaning gently and clutching his trousers. 'What'll I tell the Guv'nor? We'd better find that Formula here, or else.' He sneezed again, blowing the living room door open. 'There's no time to go after the girl now. Get in there and start looking.'

Up on the main road out of Wretchford, Eddy was leading the others to Leviticus. 'I can't believe Professor Blut is still alive! We have to tell Avril what's happened. She could be in terrible danger!'

'Are you *sure* you heard those men right, Augustus?' Wilfred puffed, looking up at Augustus, in Bonaparte's arms. 'The Professor's alive?'

'*More* heresy!' The dog's tail flicked. 'Are you questioning my imperial ears?'

'No, no, Augustus! It's just . . .w-well, I thought he was killed in that explosion in Gargoyle Woods . . .' Wilfred pushed nervously at his glasses and moved closer to Eddy, who was staring grimly ahead as they marched on. 'Are you all right?' he whispered.

'It's just that we don't have much time,' she replied in a low voice, holding her left hand up for Wilfred to see in the dawn light. 'Look.'

10

Wilfred stared at the purple number. He was starting to feel useless.

'We just have to hope Avril's got a cure,' Eddy said.

'Otherwise I'll be gone before I can do *anything* to save Lionel.'

'D-don't say that, Eddy!'

'But it's true. It's already eight o'clock, and it's miles to Leviticus. If I don't stay awake the whole journey, we won't get to Leviticus in time.'

Wilfred suddenly let out a cry. 'A bus! If we cut across the moor to Puddleton, we can get one from there when they start running. It's only a few miles.'

'Good idea, Wilfred.' Eddy squeezed his mittened hand, then let out a long sigh.

'Avril *will* have a cure,' Wilfred said firmly. 'Avril w-will save you, Eddy. And w-we will get there in time.'

Eddy said nothing for a moment. Then she changed the subject. 'If we're going to cut across the moor, shouldn't we get off the main road soon?'

'Yes.' Wilfred pushed at his glasses and stared up into the sky. 'Puddleton's north-east of here. It's a good thing it's still dark enough to see the stars. And a good thing D-dad gave me all those astronomy textbooks last Christmas, even though I really wanted a puppy . . .'

'A dog is for life,' floated Augustus' disapproving voice, 'not just for Christmas.'

'Ignore him,' said Eddy, as they clambered over a hedge on to the moor. She wrapped her hand tightly around the solid form of the fob watch. 'Do you think we could go a bit faster? And – if I fall asleep before we get to Puddleton, just stay with me, would you? I don't want to be left alone . . .'

★

'*Boss . . . Boss . . . This is Red Herring. Can you hear me?*'

In Lab 100, Gideon snatched at the air close to where his radio lay. His eyes were clouding over with sleep . . . he could hardly see . . .

'*Boss, we got a problem. That little girl you just told us to pick up . . .*'

Now Gideon managed to grab the radio. 'She *is* still alive?'

'*Oh, very much so, Boss.*'

'Excellent. Then bring her to . . .'

'*Least, she were good an' alive when she ran away ten minutes ago.*'

Gideon moaned into the radio.

'*Awww, Boss, it's nice to hear you so calm. We was dead worried you'd shout at us.*'

'You fools!'

'*Now, now,*' said Red Herring. '*No need for names. Not when we got you another prisoner. Bigger an' better, too. That Lionel bloke from the guesthouse. We had to give him a bit of a goin' over. He's in the back of the van now,*' he added, proudly.

'But I don't want him!' hissed Gideon. 'I want . . .'

He stopped.

Bait.

'The prisoner – Lionel. He can be of use to me after all,' Gideon said quietly into the radio. 'Bring him here at once.'

Willing his eyes to stay open, Gideon staggered across the lab to the Replication Chamber. The original Lionel would never consent to bring him the girl. But a different Lionel would.

He had one more clone to make.

12

The Great Escape

Sedukta moved towards Avril and Dr Wetherby with the syringe. 'Which of you is going to talk first?'

Dr Wetherby staggered as far back as he could, until he was pressed against Lab 99's curved white wall. 'I don't know what it is you want to hear!' he howled. 'But believe me, I'll tell you anything!'

'I want to know where Crump has hidden the Formula.'

Dr Wetherby was whimpering. 'But I don't know about any Formula . . .'

'That's good, Raymond,' hissed Avril in a very loud voice. 'Don't say anything.'

Dr Wetherby stared at her, aghast. 'What are you talking about, woman? I don't *know* anything.'

'Sure you don't, Raymond.' Avril gave him a huge theatrical wink, hoping that Sedukta would see, and shifted her rucksack ostentatiously from one shoulder to the other.

'Are you mad?' Dr Wetherby looked as if he might strangle her. 'What do you mean by pretending I know something I don't?'

'What is in that rucksack?' snapped Sedukta. She took another step towards Dr Wetherby. 'Open it at once.'

'*This* rucksack? Oh, there's nothing in here but sandwiches,' Avril said. 'Rather good peanut butter and banana ones, if I may say so. You know me, Sedukta.' She patted her significant waistline. 'Never far from a snack or two!'

'While that is all to easy to believe,' Sedukta sneered, 'I think there is something else in there, Dr Crump.'

'Have you got this Formula after all?' Dr Wetherby snatched the rucksack from Avril's shoulder.

'Open the rucksack.' Sedukta's syringe was moving closer to Dr Wetherby's arm. 'Or suffer the consequences.'

'It's not fair!' Dr Wetherby unzipped the bag with

shaking hands. '*I'm* the one being co-operative here! Can't you just inject *her* and be done with it?' He peered into the rucksack and his face fell. 'There *are* just sandwiches in here . . . and some chocolate muffins . . . ' Then he gasped with relief. 'Oh! A piece of paper! There's a piece of paper in here!'

'No, Raymond!' Avril made a great show of wringing her hands in despair. 'Don't give it to her!'

But Dr Wetherby had already handed over the piece of paper. Sedukta studied it carefully, still holding the syringe just above Dr Wetherby's arm.

'*PM = [3F+B+2S+2M+E+5.4cc] x 8.53m @ 282*,' she read. Then she held the scrap of paper up for Dr Wetherby to see. 'Well?' she hissed. 'You're the scientist. Does this look like the Formula to you?'

Dr Wetherby peered at it. 'Well, it's certainly *a* formula, that much I can tell you . . .'

'Oh, it's just an old formula for baking muffins,' Avril scoffed. Her heart was pounding.

'A *muffin formula*?' Dr Wetherby was withering. 'Just how stupid are you, Dr Crump? *Anyone* can see that this is an extremely complicated formula. I have spent more years as a senior scientist than you've had hot dinners . . .' He thought about this as Avril's

plump face gazed up at him. 'Well, maybe not *quite*
. . . but a jolly long time. And I know what I am
talking about.' He looked back at Sedukta. 'This is
what you are looking for,' he announced. 'This
is your Formula.'

'You'd better be right.' Sedukta was already
heading for the door. 'If there has been some mistake,
I will be back – and my syringe comes with me.'

She unlocked the door and left the room, locking
the door behind her. Her footsteps clicked away down
the hall.

'Quick, Raymond! We don't have much time.'

Dr Wetherby stared at Avril as she began battering
herself against the door.

'Are you completely insane, woman? First you lie
to them about not having the Formula, then you risk
an escape attempt!'

'I have no intention of sitting about waiting for
Sedukta to return after Gideon's realised what's on
that piece of paper.'

'What do you mean?'

'*You* know, Raymond. That the Formula really is
just a muffin recipe.'

Dr Wetherby's jaw fell open. 'Do you mean to say

that you have just . . . shared *baking tips* with that psychopathic killer?'

'But Raymond, I thought you knew! I thought all that rubbish about recognising a truly sophisticated formula when you saw one was just . . . well, rubbish.'

Dr Wetherby's eyes were bulging.

'Oh, Raymond! You *really* thought that was the Formula?' Avril could not help letting out a giggle.

'I see. This is the sort of thing you find hilarious, isn't it, Dr Crump? Laugh at silly old Dr Wetherby, that washed-up old has-been of a scientist.'

Avril stared at him. His mottled face was crumpling like a withered tomato.

'Tell me what you imagine Blut's response will be,' said Dr Wetherby through gritted teeth. 'Are you hoping that he will find this as amusing as you do?'

'Raymond,' Avril put a hand on his arm but it was thrown off. 'I didn't mean to laugh at you . . .'

'Perhaps the two of you can enjoy a merry exchange of rock-cake recipes and the swapping of hilarious tales about burnt Bath buns?'

'Well, that would be awfully nice, but I don't think . . .'

'No! *Neither do I!*' Dr Wetherby yelled. '*I* have a

notion that Blut and his hired assassin will come marching back here and . . . and . . .' White-faced, he sank to the floor. 'It's bad enough being locked up in a confined space with you for the second time, Dr Crump. And now I'm going to have to die with you as well!'

'Nobody's going to die.' Avril was searching for other ways to get out. 'It's going to have to be the window.'

'My poor son, little Wilfred . . .' Dr Wetherby was weeping fat tears now. 'He'll grow up without the love and compassion of a father . . .'

'Yes, well, things won't be so different for him then, will they? Pass me my rucksack, will you? There ought to be a rope somewhere in there.'

'I'll have you know that I love my son very much!' Dr Wetherby threw the rucksack at her.

'I know that, Raymond.' Avril rifled deep in the rucksack until she found the rope. 'It's just that there's more to love than helping with a Geography project.'

Dr Wetherby blinked. 'It happened to be an *excellent* Geography project – well, by the time I'd finished with it. Whatever that Dougall dumbo said!'

He stared at Avril as she looped the rope around the end of one workbench and pulled it with all her might, testing its strength. 'What *are* you doing, Dr Crump?'

'Raymond, take off your clothes.'

'I *beg* your pardon?'

'We're going to abseil out of the window and down to the lab below. It won't be locked. Now, if we tie your tracksuit to this rope, we should just make it.' Avril pulled at his tracksuit top. 'Come on! Take it off.'

'Dr Crump! Are you making Suggestions of a Lewd and Lascivious nature to a Senior Scientist? That's a breach of Rule 675, paragraph 43!'

'But you're wearing something underneath, aren't you?'

'All I have on underneath this is a light-but-surprisingly-warm thermal vest and some amusing novelty underpants. So you will have to look else-where for your abseiling equipment. Besides, where do you plan to go *after* you have pulled off this latest daredevil stunt?'

'To Lab One to find that Formula,' said Avril. 'Nobody knows that lab like I do. I bet I'll find it where they'd never even think of looking for it. Come on, Raymond! The top, at least.'

'Why can't *you* supply the clothing?' whined Dr Wetherby.

'For one thing, all my clothes will be too short. And for another . . .'

'You have a point.' Dr Wetherby began hastily unzipping his tracksuit top to reveal the white vest beneath. 'The last thing this messed-up world needs is the sight of your wobbling flesh.' Surreptitiously, he flexed a vest-clad bicep.

Avril tied one sleeve of the jacket to the rope in an elaborate knot that she remembered from her one near-fatal visit to the Girl Guides. Then she opened the window and peered down. Her stomach lurched slightly. Eleven floors was an awfully long way down if anything went wrong.

'I think I ought to go first, Dr Crump,' said Dr Wetherby. That way when – I mean *if* – you break it, at least one of us will be free.'

The rope was fastened around the table leg, and then tied securely around Dr Wetherby's waist before he clambered up on to the leather chair next to the window. There followed several minutes of safety testing before he finally pronounced himself satisfied.

'Right, Raymond. Once you've kicked through the window below and landed in the lab, chuck the rope back up to me and I'll come down to join you.' Avril pushed the window wide open. 'Are you ready?' She did not wait for his answer before giving him a smart shove off the chair. He toppled backwards out of the window.

'Aaaaaaaaaarrrgggh!' came a wail as he swung through the air, his bare arms glowing white in the early morning light. 'What did you do that for?'

'I was saving you from having to make the jump!' She jumped up on to the leather chair herself and peered out of the window. 'Are you all right down there?'

'I'm afraid of heights . . .' came a wail from a floor below.

'Then why on earth didn't you say something *before* I pushed you out of an eleventh-storey window?'

'I didn't know I was afraid of heights! Believe it or not, Dr Crump, I've never *been* pushed out of an eleventh-storey window before!'

'What, *never*?' Avril thought back to her days of human-flight experiments. Leaping out of high

111

windows had been a particular speciality until the hospital had finally refused to admit her any more. 'Come on, Raymond, we must hurry. Just try to kick that window-pane in.' She leaned out a little further. 'All you have to do is swing yourself feet first through that window. Nothing could be easier.'

From below, there was a gentle but persistent sobbing.

Avril lost her patience. 'Look, Raymond. We're running out of time! We need that Formula and we need it n . . .'

At that moment, the rope slipped and Avril lost her balance. Performing a near-perfect forward-flip, she toppled out of the window.

The ground rushed up towards her so fast that she was too shocked even to yell. Then, in mid-air, her stomach hit Dr Wetherby's right leg, which he had stuck out at a ninety-degree angle to catch her.

For a moment, neither was capable of speech. Avril hung like a folded sandwich board, gasping to get her breath back.

'Dr Crump . . .' Dr Wetherby's face was contorted. 'Is this another misguided attempt to cure my phobia? Or are you thinking of taking up sky-diving?'

'I'm sorry, Raymond!' Avril tried to haul herself into an upright position, slipped, and only managed to cling to Dr Wetherby's leg with the tips of her fingers.

'My leg!' Dr Wetherby howled. 'Do you think I'm some sort of prima ballerina?'

He did indeed look like a ballerina, silhouetted in his vest against the brightening sky with his right leg out behind him in a graceless arabesque. Avril kicked her own legs to try to haul herself upwards, but the rope made a dangerous creaking noise.

'It won't support both of us!' she gasped.

'Then get off!' Dr Wetherby kicked at her with his other leg. 'This is *my* rope. I was here first. Plunge to a messy death, can't you, and leave me be!'

'I know you don't mean that, Raymond.'

'Wrong!' Dr Wetherby looked down at her. 'Oh, all right, then. Have it your way. We'll *both* plunge to a messy death.'

'There's no need for that . . .' Avril was reaching out with her arm nearest to the building. This put a terrible strain on her other arm, still clutching Dr Wetherby's trousers. 'If I can just get to this window . . .' Just as her hand clamped securely on to the window-frame, the rope snapped.

'Raymond, I'm sorry . . .'

'Dr Crump, I love you . . .'

They plummeted at speed towards the concrete.

13

Puddleton

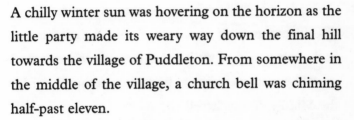

A chilly winter sun was hovering on the horizon as the little party made its weary way down the final hill towards the village of Puddleton. From somewhere in the middle of the village, a church bell was chiming half-past eleven.

'I'm so sorry,' Eddy said. Her feet were so cold that she could hardly feel the blisters from the four-mile walk. 'If I hadn't fallen asleep for so long back there, we'd have been here two hours ago.'

'That's all right, Eddy!' Wilfred grinned at her. 'As soon as w-we find a bus, we'll make up all that lost time. Besides, w-we had a great time while we w-waited, didn't we? Playing I Spy, and everything . . .' His grin froze as Augustus glared out at him from his

115

tartan blanket.

'*You* may have had a great time. *I* did not.'

'Twas yet more folly upon thy part to win each game,' Bonaparte said disapprovingly. 'Mr Dog will not deign to play with thee again.'

'Too right I won't,' Augustus snapped. He shifted rather uncomfortably in his blanket, as his stick dug into his back for the third time in as many minutes, then peered about as they tramped on down the hill. 'What's happening now?'

Eddy was still trying to shake off the feeling of disorientation from her deep sleep. 'We're going to find a bus and then we'll be on our way to Leviticus.'

'Where are we going to find a bus in this place? It's the Middle of Nowhere!'

'Nay, Mr Dog, 'tis Puddleton!' Bonaparte pointed up at a banner that someone had strung between two trees. '*Puddleton*,' he read, '*500th Jubilee Puddleball Match here today at two o'clock!*' Pray, what is this "Puddleball", Miss Eddy?'

'I don't know.'

'A mystery indeed! Mayhap we will find a kindly local soul who will answer our queries.'

'No, Bony. We're on the run, don't forget. People

116

are hunting for us.' Eddy squinted against the low sun to see if a bus stop was materialising. The winding lane into Puddleton was lined on one side with low, thatched cottages, but there was nobody in sight to ask for directions. Apart from the distant bell, the only sound was the trickling and gurgling of a stream that ran on the other side of the road, behind thick trees. 'We just want to find the bus stop and get out of here as fast as possible. You mustn't speak to *anybody*, Bony. Nor you, Gus. It could be very dangerous.'

'Not half as dangerous as you calling me Gus,' the dog said. 'Anyway, who do you imagine we're going to talk to? The place is deserted.'

'But I'm *sure* there are buses from Puddleton on Saturdays,' Wilfred was thinking aloud. 'D-dad always says he w-won't go into the shops in Wretchford on Saturdays because of all the bumpkins bussed in from Puddleton and Puddleswick.'

'What a man of charm and tact your father is.' Augustus snuggled down warmly into Bonaparte's arms again.

'Augustus, don't you dare be so rude about Wilfred's dad . . .' Eddy began, when there was a sudden noise from one of the thatched cottages on the side of the lane. A door was flung open and a group of teenage boys tumbled out. They were all wearing red and white shirts, scarves and woollen hats.

'Come on, Puddleton!' one of them yelled as they began to advance down the lane towards the centre of the village. The cry was echoed from a window of another cottage, and an even larger group of people emerged.

'The Hogmastide Pies are on me!' cried a red-and-white-clad grandmother, to cheers all round.

'Stay back!' Eddy pulled Wilfred off the road and into the thick trees opposite the cottages. 'Don't let them see us.'

'But Eddy, w-we need to ask someone if there's a bus.' Wilfred squinted ahead. 'They look perfectly safe.'

The lane was beginning to fill with more and more people, all dressed in the same colours. Wilfred was right, thought Eddy: nobody would pay much attention to them with all the excitement of this match. For once, she might even be able to blend in with ordinary people. Even Bony wouldn't stand out here in his red uniform.

'Come on. I'll ask for directions. Everybody else

just stay quiet.' The four stepped out of the trees and joined the throng on its way down the lane. Eddy put her hand in her pocket to hold on to Avril's fob watch, for luck. 'Hi, there,' she said offhandedly to a rather mournful young man sloping along the road by himself, his red-and-white scarf dragging along the ground. 'Is there a bus stop in Puddleton?'

'Yeah, there's a bus stop,' said the young man, fingering a large boil on his chin and sounding as if he were announcing the death of a much-loved pet.

'Great! Could you tell us where it is?'

'Just round this corner,' he sighed. 'See?'

Eddy followed his pointing finger. A wooden lean-to was just visible around the corner of the winding lane.

'Course, you'll be lucky if you get a bus today. All the drivers are skiving off because of the big match.'

'Match? Pray, tell us more, good fellow!' The tall clone clapped his hands excitedly, almost dropping Augustus.

'Puddleton – that's us – plays Puddleswick – that's, like, the next village – at Puddleball. Happens once a year, on Hogmastide. There's always this, like, big fete and stuff on the Village Green. That's where everyone's going now. I was s'posed to be going with my girlfriend Lucretia, but she dumped me for Baz from Puddleswick last Thursday.' The young man's face grew even longer. 'Anyway, we're just gonna lose. We always do. We've lost four hundred and ninety-nine years in a row. And this year it's, like, gonna be even more embarrassing, cos of the TV cameras and everything. It's going to be on Wretchford News Hour, you know.'

'*TV cameras.*'

'Here, you want to see someone about that.' The young man blinked at Bonaparte's apparently talking stomach in alarm before sloping off down the lane towards the Green.

'Let's move, Eddy.' Wilfred led her out of the crowd and towards a stone wall that she could lean against. The bad news about the bus drivers had seemed to drain her of energy.

'Where are the TV cameras?' Augustus was fighting to get out of Bonaparte's grip as he too was carried towards the wall. 'How's my fur, Bony? Do my ears look all right? Oh, if only I hadn't eaten all those pizzas earlier! The camera adds ten pounds, you know . . .'

'What are we going to do?' Wilfred stared at his friend, seeing her shoulders slump and her eyes grow heavy. 'We'll never walk all the way to Leviticus in time!'

'Oi! You kids! Get away from my wall!' An old man had come out of an outbuilding behind the wall and was advancing across a messy farmyard towards them. The yard was filled with mouldering bales of hay, a rusty old tractor and several large pigs. The old man was almost as thin as Bonaparte, though about a foot shorter, and wore a stained black coat down to his ankles. Greasy grey hair hung in a limp ponytail on his shoulders, and the same hair sprouted out of his nostrils and ears. A very bad smell hung about him. It had notes of manure and old cabbage soup. 'What you lot staring at?' he yelled, scooping up a handful of mud and waving it at them threateningly. 'Get out of here before I set Gormenghast on you!'

'Come on, Eddy.' Wilfred pulled at her arm, wondering which of the mean-looking porkers was Gormenghast. One in particular had a crazed look in its piggy eye. 'Let's get away from here so we can think.'

Eddy was just about to nod her weary head in agreement when a clump of earth struck her on the head.

'Oi! Little girl! Get this Puddleball-supporting lout away from me an' all!' The old man was advancing on Bonaparte, who had not followed Eddy and Wilfred away from the junkyard.

'But sir, I simply wish to be allowed to sit upon yon tractor. I have yearned for a tractor ever since I did see one upon yon television last week. Its shiny red paint did glow in the morning sunlight, its driver did give a merry wave . . .'

'Nutter!'

'Peasant!' Augustus yelled back from somewhere inside Bonaparte's grip.

Eddy saw a puzzled expression pass across the farmer's dirty face. 'Bony, come at once!' She pulled him away before Augustus could say another word. 'Look, we can't waste time here any longer. We've got to find another way to get to Leviticus.'

'I'm so sorry about the buses, Eddy.' Wilfred stared mournfully at the bus-stop. 'I should have remembered the Hogmastide match.'

But Eddy was starting to feel her eyelids growing

heavy. She glanced down at her left hand and saw the number as it changed.

6

Wilfred did not notice that Eddy's eyes were closing, or that she sat down very suddenly on the grassy roadside, and curled her legs up under her. 'We need some form of transport, or we'll never make it . . . W-what shall we do, Eddy?' He stared at her, lying on the grass verge, her eyes shut tight in her waxen face. 'Please, Eddy, not now . . .'

But Eddy did not move.

'It's no good. Who knows how long she'll sleep for this time?' Wilfred looked at the anxious faces of Augustus and Bonaparte. 'W-what are we going to *d-do*?'

Bonaparte sniffed sadly. 'I know not. Tis always *Miss Eddy* who doth tell us what we must do.'

'Hey!' Augustus flicked his tail. 'We're not incapable of doing things without old Bossy-Boots.'

Bonaparte blinked. 'Are we not?'

'Well, *I'm* certainly not incapable. I simply choose to put my enormous brain to more important matters.'

'Indeed, Mr Dog! Like yon difficult decision of whether to order additional ham atop thy pizza!'

Augustus narrowed his eyes. '*Other things too.*'

Bonaparte nodded vigorously. 'Or additional pineapple,' he agreed.

'The point *is*,' – shifting again beneath his blanket in some discomfort, Augustus looked over at Wilfred – 'that *you* have to come up with the plan.'

'W-well . . . I . . .'

'Mr Dog!' Bonaparte hissed, as Wilfred began to sweat and push at his glasses. 'Art thou certain that Young Master Wilfred is not too simple for such a task?'

Wilfred hardly heard Bonaparte. 'We're going to have to steal that old man's tractor.'

Augustus' jaw dropped. 'I am *shocked*,' he said. 'Shocked and appalled . . .'

'Shame on thee, Young Master Wilfred!'

'. . . that I didn't think of this first.' Augustus bestowed an approving gaze on the bewildered boy for the first time. 'Go forth, Wilfred, and do your worst. In the absence of a chauffeur-driven Rolls-Royce, a tractor will have to do.' He leaned closer. 'Of course, if at a later stage, we happen to come across a Rolls-Royce, don't hesitate to pinch that as well.'

'Stealing is wrong . . .' Augustus' enthusiasm was

giving Wilfred second thoughts. 'And D-dad would *kill* me if he found out.' He glanced down at Eddy. 'But we haven't got very long . . .' He took a deep breath. 'I can d-do this. I know I can.'

'Of course thou canst, Young Master Wilfred!'

'All right.' Wilfred's legs were shaking as he turned around and set off towards the farmyard. 'I'll be as quick as I can. If Gormenghast the killer pig d-doesn't get me, that is.'

Augustus waved his long tail at Wilfred. 'Chill out, kid.'

'Indeed! Do not become overheated,' Bonaparte called in agreement with Augustus as Wilfred disappeared around the bend in the lane.

'Right.' Augustus was already hopping up and down with excitement. 'Let's carry Eddy down to the stream. She'll be safe there for a few minutes.'

'Righty-ho, Mr Dog!' Bonaparte stooped to pick Eddy up, then paused. 'Forgive my ignorance, Mr Dog, but why must we do this?'

'My television debut, Bony! The TV cameras on the village Green! *Do* try to keep up!' Augustus' sharp eyes suddenly spotted Eddy shivering in her sleep and he wriggled to throw off his precious tartan blanket.

'This grotty old thing will look terrible on TV. Can't you sling it over Eddy or something?'

'An excellent suggestion, Mr Dog. And so selfless.'

'We'll only be ten minutes.' Augustus looked uncertain for a moment. 'Nothing can possibly happen to her. Can it?'

'Thou knowest best, Mr Dog.' Bonaparte reached down to unwrap Augustus' blanket. As he removed it from the dog's back, the large, knobbled stick fell to the floor at his feet. 'Thou hast dropped thy precious stick, Mr Dog.'

'What?' Augustus stared down at the stick. He thought fast. 'Er – that's not my stick, Bony.'

'But 'twas beneath thy blanket, Mr Dog.'

'That may very well be, but it's not *mine*.' Augustus was starting to perspire. 'Eddy just put it there for protection. It's not like I'm some common stick-loving canine. You'll be buying me chew-toys next!'

'Indeed not, Mr Dog! Fear not, for I shall throw away this offending item.' He hurled the knobbly stick through the air, watching it with satisfaction as it fell . . . fell . . . towards a bright yellow Mini that was stalling and bunny-hopping its way down the lane towards them.

'Brilliant, Bony!' Augustus cringed as the stick hit the car's bonnet, causing it to screech to a halt, one wheel up on the kerb. 'Now we'll have to do a runner.'

Bonaparte was already running – towards the car. He had recognised it immediately, and was whooping with joy as he ran.

'I don't believe it,' said Augustus, as the driver clambered out of the Mini, entangled in a giant, unfolded road map. *'Lionel?'*

14

Gormenghast

'. . . and when I woke up, I was tied up in the coal cellar. I shouted myself hoarse until the neighbours heard and let me out, then I leapt in the car for Leviticus.' Lionel's clone was doing some fast thinking. Sedukta, who had a fondness for anagrams, had given him the codename O'Neill. She had also given him his cover story for the moment he found the clones, and now he was struggling to recall it. 'Er – oh, yes!' he remembered, still disentangling himself from the ardent embrace of the huge road map. I always suspected that Blut was still alive, and his thugs simply confirmed my suspicions. I'm not going to let him get away with all this!'

'What are you going to *do*?' asked Augustus

dubiously. 'Ram-raid Leviticus in your Mini and take him prisoner? Threaten him with suffocation by road map?'

'Yes, well, I haven't got an *exact* plan,' said O'Neill, turning rather red and finally flinging off the enormous map. He stamped on it several times for good measure, before it could rise up and attack him once more. 'But what a good thing I *was* going to Leviticus! You clones need my help!'

'That's debatable,' said Augustus. 'Anyway, if it's Leviticus you want, you do realise that you're heading in the wrong direction. You were driving towards Crumpy's house.'

O'Neill's mouth flapped open like a fish. 'Yes . . . er . . .'

'Oh, Mr Lionel!' Bonaparte shrieked. 'I have worked it all out!'

'*What?*' O'Neill held up his hands. 'Now, I can explain . . .'

'Thou art so enamoured of thy dear Lady Avril, that thou art simply drawn towards her abode, no matter where thy brain tells thee thou must go!' Bonaparte sighed happily.

'Yes! That's it!' said O'Neill, as Augustus snorted.

'I *was* driving to Leviticus, but somehow I found myself drawn back towards Avril's house! I can't explain it.'

'For who *can* explain,' declaimed Bonaparte, 'where Cupid's arrow doth fall?'

'Stupid's arrow, more like,' said Augustus.

O'Neill stared down at Eddy, still sleeping by the roadside. 'So how long do we have?'

'I do believe it is no more than five hours,' said Bonaparte sadly, gazing at Eddy's left hand on top of the blanket.

'Then we must hurry. I just hope I can get my car to start.' O'Neill was starting to feel desperate. *Got to get the girl away from these two before they suspect anything . . .*

'Young Master Wilfred – though tragically a poor fool – doth claim to be knowledgeable in all matters pertaining to engine craft.'

'He means,' Augustus translated wearily, seeing Lionel's uncomprehending stare, 'that Wilfred can fix cars.'

O'Neill blinked, racking his brain for any information he had on someone called Wilfred. It rang only the faintest of bells. 'But who *is* this Wilfred?'

'You remember – Eddy's pal from St Swithin's School for the Terminally Talentless. The one with the specs.' Augustus was trotting over to the car to pick up his stick. Furtively, he inspected it for damage. 'He's stealing a tractor at that farmyard down the road.'

'Stealing a *tractor*?' The last thing O'Neill needed was a crime being committed. If the police showed up, they would never let him take the sleeping girl away. 'But he could get arrested for that!'

'He *should* get arrested for barefaced heresy,' Augustus said, 'but if you can arrange it on another charge, that's fine by me.'

An idea came to O'Neill, one that would leave him free of the talking dog, the weird Shakespearean beanpole and the nuisance boy in one fell swoop. 'Right. Here's the plan. I'll go and get Wilfred, he can fix my engine, and we'll leave for Leviticus right away!'

'All right,' said Augustus. 'You'll be back in about ten minutes, will you?'

'Er . . . even faster, I hope!'

'No, no,' Augustus said firmly. 'Ten minutes will be just fine.' He could hear the music on the Green. There was still time to make it to the cameras.

The pigs were circling the tractor, watching Wilfred as he finished off his repairs to the ancient engine with a spanner he had found in the nearby shed.

'Apple sauce,' he hissed at them when their dripping snouts got too close. He was just about to clamber up into the grimy cabin and see if he could start the engine when the slamming of a door made him glance up.

The farmer had come out of the outbuilding opposite.

'Gormy!' he shouted. 'Oh, Gormenghast!'

Wilfred leapt off the step and ducked down behind the tractor. Pigs clustered around him in an instant. 'Apple sauce,' he hissed his mantra. 'Apple sauce!'

'Where's my boy?' Wilfred heard him call. 'Come to Daddy!'

The pigs moved closer to Wilfred, squealing in terror.

Then Wilfred heard a dog bark.

'That's my boy! Good Gormy. Good dog.'

Wilfred peeped around the tractor's grille. The sight before his eyes almost made him fall over.

'*Augustus?*' he gasped.

A large, floppy-eared, mud-coloured dog was standing in the middle of the courtyard.

Wilfred peered at it, pushing his glasses up his nose for a closer squint. It was not actually Augustus. On second viewing, this dog's coat shone with the signs of the regular grooming that Augustus spurned. He was also perhaps an inch or two slimmer around the middle.

'Hungry, Gormy? Want a snack?' The farmer stood up. 'You bring home the bacon!'

Suddenly, Gormenghast set back his ears and howled. Now any trace of resemblance to Augustus was gone. His mouth was drawn back, displaying knife-sharp teeth dripping with expectant saliva, and his eyes were filled with what Wilfred, no dog psychiatrist, could only interpret as blood-lust.

The howling set the pigs scattering like machine-gun fire all over the yard, squealing as Gormenghast ran at them. Wilfred was frozen for a moment, until his shaking legs fled for the shed behind him. He shut the door tight. Out of the tiny window he could see that Gormenghast had selected a victim. Wilfred regretted every 'apple sauce' he had recently uttered with all his heart as he watched the dog circle the petrified creature. But there was no time for regrets – the farmer, who had been watching the sport with a grin, was now striding towards Wilfred's hiding place.

Wilfred dived for the narrow gap between a locked cupboard and the shed wall, and squeezed himself as far back as it was possible to go. The space was so narrow that he could feel the splintery wood of the cupboard in his back with every outward breath.

Wilfred did not move. At the shed door, he heard a clink of metal, and then a snap.

'That shouldn't have been open,' the farmer muttered to himself, and crunched his way back across the yard. 'Good boy, Gormy!' he called over the pig's screams. 'Save some for Daddy!'

Wilfred was close to tears. He was locked in! Edging out of his hiding place, he rattled at the handle on the inside of the door, but it did not give an inch. Through the tiny window, he caught a glimpse of Gormenghast, dragging the pig out of the back of the yard with the strength of a dog three times his size. But it was the sight across the other side of the yard, near the road, that gave him a bigger jolt. The farmer was talking to somebody over the stone wall.

Lionel! Wilfred was about to bang his fists on the glass when he heard Lionel speak.

'If you see him, keep him out of my way.'

Wilfred almost didn't recognise the hard expression on Lionel's face as he handed the farmer a large wad of ten-pound notes.

'Remember,' he heard Lionel say, 'he's about ten years old, wears spectacles. He's here somewhere. Now, the other two are out in the lane. Tall, thin fellow and a dog. I want you to take care of them, too. There'll be more money in it.'

Wilfred's jaw dropped. Why would Lionel want him out of the way? He had to warn Eddy that Lionel was not a friend after all. He stared about the shed, discounting the tiny window once more. Then he saw it. In the wall behind him was a gap between two rotting planks of wood. It was only about a centimetre wide, but it ran all the way down from the ceiling to the floor. If he could make it wider, just wide enough for a hand to slip through, he might be on to something.

He reached for the spanner in his duffle coat pocket, and began carving.

'When one door closes, another one opens.'

15

Mr Odorous Faintly-Whiffy

'Careful, Bony! Put her somewhere dry or she'll freeze.'

Bonaparte carefully placed Eddy on the bank of the stream. 'Perhaps we could leave thy stick beside her for protection.'

'*No!* What would dozy old Eddy want with a stick?' Augustus handed the stick up to Bonaparte between his teeth. 'You hold on to it, Bony, just in case we change our minds about its utter uselessness. But be careful with it!'

'Very well, Mr Dog.' Bonaparte stuffed the stick inside his red jacket, then proceeded to rearrange the tartan blanket over Eddy.

'There's no time for that! The quicker we go, the

quicker we're back. We don't want Lionel to know about this.' Augustus cast a glance over his shoulder at the slumbering Eddy as he and Bonaparte bounded back up through the trees to the road. 'She'll be perfectly all right, won't she?'

'I am sure of it, Mr Dog. 'Twill be but a few minutes of separation. And she will be overcome with delight to hear about thy Big Break.'

An expression of horror passed across Augustus' face as the pair began hurrying down the road towards the Green. 'Er, let's keep this to ourselves, shall we, Bony? I'm not sure Eddy will see my television career in quite the positive light that she ought to.'

But Bonaparte was not paying attention. 'Today, Wretchford News Hour, tomorrow, thy own show. There shall be opening credits to the simple tune of My Name is Mr Dog . . . Perhaps,' he added shyly, 'I might be blessed with a part to play in thy television debut?'

'Of course.' Augustus waved a bountiful paw. 'There are a lot of cut-throat people in showbiz, Bony. I shall need someone trustworthy to handle my pizza orders.'

'Oh, Mr Dog! How can I ever thank thee enough?'

Augustus suddenly sniffed the air and wrinkled his nose in distaste as a terrible aroma filled his nostrils. 'You can start by keeping that pong to yourself, thank you.

Bonaparte had also noticed the smell. His eyes were beginning to water. 'But I did think that 'twas *thee*, Mr Dog, and thy' – he lowered his voice confidentially – 'over-sensitive aristocratic digestion!'

Augustus stopped and glowered at Bonaparte. 'If you mention that cauliflower stew *one more time*,' he began, when a footfall some distance behind caught his attention. He turned round. The old farmer was following them. '*He's* the stinky one, Bony!' hissed Augustus as the farmer approached. 'Get rid of him, quick!'

'Not going to the match, then?' the farmer grimaced at them as he approached, displaying stained yellow teeth.

'No,' Bonaparte said stiffly. 'We have no time for Puddleball today.'

'Your dog want a biscuit or summat?'

Bonaparte frowned. 'No, indeed. Mr Dog doth not sully his fine palate with *biscuits*. Besides, poor quality goods produce the most terrible reaction from his over-sensitive aristocratic digest . . .'

Augustus picked up a pebble with the tip of his tail and flung it at Bonaparte's shins.

'Obadiah Grimley-Stenching,' growled the farmer suddenly.

'I beg thy pardon?'

'Obadiah Grimley-Stenching. That's my name.'

'There's a surprise,' Augustus muttered beneath his breath,

'Funny-looking dog you got there,' Obadiah said. 'If I didn't know I was on me way *to* the pub and not on the way *back*, I'd say he was talking. His mouth moves all peculiar.'

'How darest thou, Mr Odorous Faintly-Whiffy!' said Bonaparte. 'Mr Dog's mouth doth not "move all peculiar". Why, he is the most handsome and distinguished rare breed of Tor Kin Wan ever to grace us with his presence!'

'Too right I am,' said Augustus.

Obadiah Grimley-Stenching let out a startled wheeze. O'Neill had not mentioned this! 'Bloomin' Nora! The dog talks!' He could hardly believe his luck. *All those ten-pound notes, and the opportunity of a lifetime* . . . He licked his lips and stared at Augustus. 'Talking mutt like that, he should be on television!'

'Television . . .' Augustus breathed.

'Why, Mr Faintly-Whiffy, that is where we are transporting ourselves at this very moment.' Bonaparte gestured excitedly in the direction of the Green.

'Well, it just so happens, I can help you there. TV vans are parked in my backyard,' he lied, jabbing a thumb over his shoulder. 'So why don't you come along with me? I got a nice comfortable place you can wait. Even watch me own TV if you like – hundreds of channels I've got, great big wide screen . . .'

'Lead on, yokel!' Augustus glanced over to the trees in front of Eddy's resting-place. 'But we can't possibly be any longer than ten minutes, do you understand? Those TV people will be begging me for more, but they'll simply have to join the queue.'

'Oh, I understand,' said Obadiah Grimley-Stenching. And he smiled. 'You two come along wi' me.'

16

Fancy Dress

For a moment, Avril thought she must be on a beach in Hawaii. A faint whooshing sound brought back many happy memories of her Crump Oscillating Wave Column experiments in Honolulu. Then she realised that it was a freezing cold wind, and not the sound of the sea. She blinked to clear her vision. She was inside a huge builder's skip, outside Leviticus, and the sun was shining.

How many hours had passed since they had plunged out of the eleventh-storey window? Avril's watch had been smashed by the fall and she was too confused and giddy to work out the time by the position of the sun. Far easier to listen to her stomach, where the particular ferocity of growling could only mean one thing: lunch-time. Avril stretched her battered limbs and suppressed a brief but powerful longing for an enormous jam sandwich and a glass of chocolate milk.

Then she remembered.

Edna.

'Raymond, we have to get back into Leviticus and find the Formula! Edna's time is running out! Raymond?' She hauled herself up to look right over the edge of the skip. If he had just missed her landing-place by a couple of metres, he would have hit the rock-hard concrete instead of uncomfortable but cushioning builder's junk. But there was no sign of him anywhere outside the skip.

'Raymond, I know you're upset with me about the fall, but please come out! There's no time to sulk.' Avril began hurling bricks and plaster out of the skip, desperate to find him in the rubble.

Then she felt a tap on her shoulder, turned around and screamed.

A giant rat was sitting in the far corner of the skip.

It was even bigger than Goliath the Gargantuan, a rat Avril had once rescued from the Food Scientists' lab. It was, in fact, even bigger than a small-to-medium Food Scientist. And it was waving.

'Get this thing off my head,' the rat suddenly yelled. 'I can't breathe, I can't see . . .'

'*Raymond?*' Avril decided that he must have died and, in a fitting twist of karma, come back as a rat. 'Oh, Raymond, this is all my fault!'

'Too right it's all your fault, missy! And I shall be having stiff words with those unemployed actors as well. How dare they throw out their costumes like this! I paid good money to hire these.'

'Oh, it's a *costume* . . .' Avril scrambled to her feet, nearly slipping as relief made her legs wobble.

'Well, of course it's a costume!' The rat folded his arms irritably. 'You didn't think I'd died and, in a fitting twist of karma, come back as a rat, did you?'

Avril gave a nervous laugh as she began pulling at the giant rat head on Dr Wetherby's shoulders. 'Oh, no, Raymond! Besides, if you died and came back as anything, I'm sure it would be something terribly dignified.'

Avril managed to get a firm hold on the dust-covered synthetic fur and fell backwards as she pulled the head off. 'Now, Raymond, what's the time?'

Dr Wetherby stared down at his watch. 'Two o'clock,' he said.

'*Two* o'clock?' Avril began clambering across the rubbish to reach the edge of the skip. 'I promised the clones I'd be back with a cure *hours* ago . . .'

'Dr Crump, you gave Blut a muffin recipe in place of his Formula. He will be looking everywhere for us . . .' He was pale and sweating, despite the extreme cold and the fact that he was only wearing a vest on his top half. 'As a senior scientist, I forbid this!'

'Blut might be looking for us, but I have to risk it. I need the Formula!'

'It's not just Blut.' Dr Wetherby pulled her back again. 'If the Governors find out I am here, I will be in very big trouble.'

'What on earth do you mean?'

'I was sacked two weeks ago. My Christmas Science for Kids initiative was, not to put too fine a point on it, a total disaster. A week of educational fun turned into what can only be described as Santagate.'

'Santagate?'

Dr Wetherby sighed. His stiff shoulders were slumped now, and he did not look at Avril, hanging half-in and half-out of the skip. 'In my final Christmas lecture I was going to explain, in scientific terms, how Santa Claus can fly around the planet in a single night.

Then Santa was supposed to arrive on a specially-built electric sleigh and hand out suitably educational gifts.'

'*Educational* gifts? Couldn't Santa just have given them toy sports-cars and lemonade-filled water pistols?'

'Santa didn't have time to give them any gifts *at all*,' said Dr Wetherby. 'Santa's sleigh blew up.'

'You blew up Santa's sleigh? With Santa *in* it?'

'*It was an actor!*' Dr Wetherby snapped. 'And he was quite all right once we'd got him down from the floor above. Honestly, Dr Crump, I hardly wish to be lectured on the perils of explosions by *you*, of all people. The children were *supposed* to find it entertaining. Instead, several ended up in hospital with shock.' He suddenly seemed to feel the biting wind, and shivered violently. 'They sacked me on the spot, after twenty years of loyal service. I am nothing without my job, Dr Crump. That is why I sneak in to work on my intermetallic powders in the Animal Storage Room late at night, when there are no guards around to see me on the CCTV. And that is why I cannot come and find your Formula with you.'

Avril put a hand on his arm. 'I'm sorry, Raymond.'

Dr Wetherby did not shake off her hand. 'I can't

tell Wilfred I've lost my job. What will he think of me?'

'He'll think you're wonderful,' said Avril. 'Like he already does.'

Dr Wetherby blinked at her. 'I beg your pardon.'

But an idea had just struck Avril. 'I wonder if Santa's costume has been dumped in here too.' She rummaged around, and produced an enormous pair of scarlet trousers, a long, white fluffy beard and a red jacket with ermine-trimmed, slightly explosion-damaged hood. 'This is our way into Leviticus. Gideon will never know it's us, and the official guards watching the CCTV won't recognise you, so you won't get in any trouble!'

Dr Wetherby stared at her. 'You propose that we *put on fancy dress*?'

'If anyone asks, we're just a couple of lost actors.' Avril was already pulling on the Santa costume. 'Shame there isn't a lovely present-stuffed sack,' she said wistfully. 'Come on then, Raymond! We have to make up for lost time.'

'This is all very well,' Dr Wetherby glared at her. 'But what do *I* wear?'

'The rat, of course.' Avril swung herself out of the skip to pull on the trousers. 'Just find the matching bottom half and we're away!'

Dr Wetherby picked up the rat head. 'But there isn't a matching bottom half. That was another thing that upset the children. The costume order went wrong and I ended up with a half-rat-half-mermaid. The parents thought I was advocating genetic modification of small furry animals. And mermaids.'

'Come *on*, Raymond!' said Avril.

'But *you've* got a proper costume.' Dr Wetherby was sulking. 'I don't want to be a Mer-Rat. It'll look stupid.' He rummaged in the skip and brought out a long, turquoise mermaid tail, covered with spangles that caught the light.

'Well, look on the bright side, Raymond,' Avril said as he pulled it on over his tracksuit bottoms with a scowl. 'Nobody will recognise you in a million years. Now, are we ready?'

'If we must.'

'Then let's go. Oh, and by the way, Raymond, about that confession of love . . .'

'Confession of *what*?' Dr Wetherby had put his rat head on again and his voice was muffled.

'As we fell. You said you loved me. But don't worry, Raymond. I'm rather flattered. There's no need to be embarrassed.'

Dr Wetherby's rat head fell off. His mouth was open. 'I never said anything of the . . . well, it must have been the stress of imminent death! I certainly didn't mean . . .'

'If you say so, Raymond.'

'I *do* say so. I find you physically appalling, woman, had you forgotten?'

'Oh.' Avril was rather hurt. 'Perhaps it's my sparkling personality, then.'

Dr Wetherby howled with laughter.

'See? I make you laugh, don't I?' Avril beamed at him.

'I am laughing *at* you, Dr Crump. Not *with* you.'

There was a pause.

'I didn't mean . . . What I meant was . . .'

'That's all right, Raymond.' Avril did not look at him as she pulled the oak door open. 'We have to get this right, Raymond. And we need that Formula. Ready?'

The Mer-Rat nodded. 'Ready.'

17

Stalker

'Like I said, we've only got ten minutes, so if you wouldn't mind being as quick as possible . . .' Augustus called after Obadiah Grimley-Stenching.

The farmer shut the door and turned a key.

'Hey! He's locked us in, Bony!'

'I am sure that it is for thy own security, Mr Dog. We do not want thee to be besieged by adoring fans.'

'True, Bony, true.' Augustus looked about the farmer's dingy front room, his eyes rapidly adjusting to the gloom.

The walls were covered with peeling orange paper, the floor was covered with stained and cracked tiles, and there were large mouse-holes in the skirting. Augustus peered up on to a wooden table at one end of the room and sniffed in disgust at the leftovers of Obadiah Grimley-Stenching's breakfast.

'This is appalling!'

'I agree, Mr Dog, but it is most considerate of Mr Faintly-Whiffy to have prepared so thoroughly for thy visit.'

'What are you talking about, Bony?' Augustus was momentarily distracted by the sight of a mouse running across the wooden tabletop. He let out an excited, involuntary bark, before hastily composing himself and making for a rocking chair in the corner. 'The man didn't even know I was coming until five minutes ago. And if he *had* known, I'd have expected a little more preparation. Fresh flowers, iced water, hot pizza . . .'

'. . . a life-sized portrait and extensive shrine . . .'

'. . . a life-sized portrait and extensive shrine . . .' Augustus stopped arranging himself on the rocking chair and thought about this. 'Actually, Bony, that would be a little creepy.'

'I confess I am in agreement with thee, Mr Dog, though we cannot blame Mr Faintly-Whiffy for trying.'

'What do you mean?'

'Behold,' said Bonaparte, pointing at the wall opposite Augustus.

There, framed in gold, was a portrait of a dog. Lovingly painted in luscious shades of muddy brown, its floppy ears lifting in some imaginary breeze, the animal gazed proudly down at them.

'Tis *thee*, Mr Dog . . .' breathed Bonaparte.

Augustus' jaw fell open and his tongue lolled in shock.

'And a series of extremely natty photographs' said Bonaparte, lifting up some smaller gilt frames on a table beneath the portrait, and tripping over something he had not seen on the floor. 'Oh! A comfortable bed, all made ready for thee!'

Beneath the portrait and the photographs, was a huge dog-bed. It was stuffed with plump velvet cushions, several cuddly and squeaky toy pigs and a soft pink cashmere blanket. This was turned back invitingly, made ready for use.

Augustus let out a frightened wheeze, all his throat was capable of. 'We've been tricked, Bony! He's not going to get us on TV at all. *He's my stalker.*'

Bonaparte had not taken his eyes off the portrait.

''Tis a splendid likeness, Mr Dog.'

'This was on that soap opera only the other day! Diavola was kidnapped by McTavish, the evil Highland baron who's been stalking her for months, and forced to marry him in his crumbling Highland lair.' The rocking-chair Augustus sat on had begun to rock back and forth in his distress, alarming him even more as he realised he could not get off. 'Help me, Bony,' he shrieked. 'This chair's been cursed!'

'Fear not, Mr Dog!' Bonaparte flung himself at the rocking chair and battered at it with his fists, only causing it to rock all the more violently until finally it flung Augustus off into a shaken, miserable heap on the floor. 'Mr Dog! Art thou all right?'

'No, Bony. I'm *all wrong*. Of all the stalkers in all the world,' moaned Augustus faintly from his heap, 'why does *mine* have to be the one with the personal hygiene problem . . .?'

'I do not wish to alarm thee, Mr Dog, but we are trapped.' Bonaparte was pulling fruitlessly at the locked door. 'There is no hope of escape, no likelihood of release, no chance,' he suddenly howled, 'of freedom!'

'I'd like to hear what you'd say if you *were* trying to alarm me. What are we going to *do*?' Augustus hissed, scrambling to his feet.

Bonaparte thought about this. 'I have only one suggestion, Mr Dog.'

'Quick! Let's hear it.'

'Thou must refuse any offers of marriage. That is my assessment of our current predicament, Mr Dog. Though it is, I am sure, a poor one.'

'No, Bony, not at all.'

'I thank thee, Mr Dog.'

'It's not just poor, Bony, it's positively destitute! A partially-trained baboon could have come up with a better plan that that!'

'But Mr Dog, that is why I am so grateful for thy noble presence. I can hardly wait to hear of thy very own plan for action! No destitute baboons there, I am sure of it!'

Augustus let out a low howl, turned his back on his horrifying shrine and began to sniff along the wall where it joined the floor. 'We'll have to take up these tiles and dig our way out,' he said. 'It's our only hope.'

'But Mr Dog, thy aristocratic paws – as featured rather fetchingly in yon sinister portrait – are far too delicate for such a task!'

'Which is why,' Augustus waved his tail, '*you* will be digging on my behalf.'

''Twould be an honour, Mr Dog!' Bonaparte pulled up two loose tiles beside the door and began to dig with his bare hands, 'If we escape from this prison, perhaps we may flee upon yon tractor. I did see it still there in yon yard, though sadly there was no sign of Young Master Wilfred. I do believe that the young fellow hath delusions of competency.' Bonaparte wiped his forehead, already beginning to sweat.

'I knew he'd never start it. Anyway, we've got Lionel to drive us now.'

At the mention of Lionel's name, Bonaparte's shining forehead creased into a frown. 'I have been pondering this matter, Mr Dog. As heartily glad as I was to see dear Mr Lionel, is't not odd that he did not re-appear with Young Master Wilfred?'

'What are you saying, Bony?'

'I know not what it is that troubles me,' Bonaparte shrugged. 'But Mr Lionel did not come back to us, and this terrible stalking man did instead.'

'Oh, don't be so paranoid, Bony!' Augustus snapped. 'Lionel's our friend.'

'Indeed, Mr Dog, but I do recall that once we did mistakenly believe a person to be Lady Avril when in fact she was a terribly evil clone.'

'Which is precisely why I shall never make that mistake again,' said Augustus. 'A Tor Kin Wan of my talents could tell if Lionel was a clone in the blink of an eye.'

'I am most glad of it, Mr Dog! What would I ever do without thee?' Relieved that his anxiety about Lionel's disappearance was unfounded, Bonaparte put his back into digging with renewed vigour.

'That's it, Bony! Dig! Dig for freedom!'

18

Old Lady, New Hope

The first thing Eddy knew was that she was very cold. The sun seemed to be shining, glowing pink inside her eyelids, but her limbs ached with a deep chill. There was something scratchy against her skin, and as she opened her eyes she saw that this was from Augustus' tartan blanket, which was wrapped around her. She kicked her legs to free them, the movement warming her frozen body, then clambered painfully to her feet like an old lady, and stretched sore arms above her head before looking around.

'That's weird . . .'

She was beside the fast-flowing stream, beneath a bank of trees that shielded her from the road. As she felt the lukewarm sensation of her blood beginning to move sluggishly around her veins, she picked up the scratchy blanket, wrapped it around her shoulders and began to wander up through the trees towards the road to tell the others she was awake.

But all Eddy could see was the empty lane and a yellow Mini, like Lionel's, parked on the kerb a few feet away.

'Wilfred, where are you?' She wandered out into the deserted lane and stared up and down it. From one direction came a distant sound of cheering and shouting – 'Puddleball,' she remembered – and from the other simply the chilly trickling of the stream.

'Augustus? Bony? I'm awake now. We really must be on our way . . .'

Eddy fumbled beneath the blanket in her pocket for the old fob watch, flipped open the battered bronze lid and stared down at its face.

'*Half-past two . . .*'

And worse, on her left hand, was the number she did not want to see. It was a single digit now . . .

4

Eddy stuffed her hand back into her pocket, clutching the fob watch so tightly that her palm hurt, and retreated back to safety behind the trees.

'Come on, Wilfred,' she murmured under her breath. 'Please . . . please . . .'

★

'They've really left me.'

For the last twenty minutes, Eddy had jumped up at every sound she had heard coming from the road. But Wilfred, Augustus and Bonaparte were nowhere to be seen.

What was she to do now? Lie down by the stream to die? Wiping away her tears, Eddy put her hand into her pocket and brought out the fob watch. For a moment, she thought she could see Avril's face reflected back at her. '*You keep an eye on that watch-face, Edna, and remember I'll be back in no time at all.*'

She couldn't give up now.

'There is a cure and it's at Leviticus.' Eddy got to her feet, throwing off the tartan blanket, and began to clamber up the steep bank to the roadside. 'I have to keep going.' She glanced down at the number on her left hand. 'Still four, still four.' But Leviticus was several miles away, across a moor that Eddy did not know how to navigate.

Then she heard an engine. A vehicle was speeding towards her, from the direction the clones had walked in.

'A *bus*?' She ran towards the bus stop, but the driver did not stop.

The young man who had told them there would be no bus drivers today had made a mistake! The bus was heading in the direction Eddy wanted to go, and now she could hear that it was slamming on its brakes, ready to slow down for the bus stop. Eddy began to run towards it. But no passengers got off, so the bus lurched back out into the road.

'Please! Wait there!'

The bus driver was visible now, shaking his head firmly at the brown-haired little girl, running breathlessly towards him. 'Missed it, love!' he yelled out of his window. 'You can only get on at the stop. Now get out of the road!' His horn blared.

'But it's an emergency . . .'

'Move! Do you want to get killed or something?'

Eddy stared as the bus as it rumbled towards her. If she didn't move, he would have to stop . . . he would have to . . . As the driver slammed on his brakes, several pebbles hit Eddy in the face, and she stumbled off the road. The fob watch spun out of her hand and hit the ground.

'Weird kid,' yelled the driver, revving his engine again and pulling away before Eddy had even taken her hands off her face. 'Go back home!'

And the bus roared away, on the road to Leviticus.

Blood trickling from her lip, Eddy scrambled to pick up the fob watch where it lay in the road. But as she flipped the lid open, all she could see was crumbled shards of glass. The watch-face was shattered, and the hands were stopped, uselessly, at six minutes and twenty-nine seconds to three. It was broken.

'It's over,' she whispered. 'It's all over.'

Her knees wobbled with each step as she walked back down to the stream, the only place her weary legs seemed willing to take her. As she reached the damp, muddy bank, feeling the ground squelch and shift beneath her feet, Eddy stared down into the stream. She could just see a quivering reflection of her face, bobbing up and down in the fast-moving water. Her eyes were wide with exhaustion and her hair was wild and uncombed. The blood on her mouth was starting to dry, but she made no move to wash it off.

'It's all over,' she whispered again, staring down at the useless, ugly fob watch in her hand. Then she stretched her arm out over the stream, and let the watch go. 'I'm sorry, Avril,' she said. 'But I just want to go to sleep now.' She sat down on the muddy ground as the watch bobbed for a moment and then sank from view. Then she rested her head on her arms and closed her eyes, waiting for the glorious warmth and comfort of sleep to embrace her one last time . . .

'You all right, girlie?'

The voice came from the other side of the stream. Eddy lifted her head and stared over to the other bank, surprised she had not seen anyone there before. A woman was sitting, like Eddy, on the muddy ground, her arms clasping her knees. Her hair was bright white and almost down to her waist, and her face was grooved with wrinkles so deep that the skin fell around them in soft folds. A gnarled hand was shielding her eyes from the bright winter sunshine as she gazed over the sparkling water.

'Everything all right?' she called again in her cracked voice. 'You don't seem to be enjoying this beautiful day, if you don't mind me saying.'

Eddy stared at her. 'I'm fine,' she replied, willing the old woman to walk away and leave her to sleep in peace.

The woman smiled, kindly, with almost toothless gums. 'Lovely young soul like you, ought to be out enjoying yourself.'

Eddy felt a lump in her throat.

'Having a bad day, are you?'

'You could say that.' Eddy's voice was very small. 'As a matter of fact, today's the last day I've got left. And they all left me alone.'

The old woman lowered her hand and looked directly at Eddy across the stream. 'I'm sorry to hear that.'

Eddy shrugged. 'That's OK. I just wish I wasn't letting Avril down. But all I want to do now is sleep.'

The old woman said nothing for a moment. Then she lifted her hand to shield her eyes again. 'I'm sorry for your friend Avril too. Sounds like you're giving up on her.'

'But what can I do?' Eddy raised her voice. 'My friends left me . . . and I missed the only bus . . . and then the watch broke . . .'

The old woman reached into the folds of her

blanket. 'Oh. Would this be your watch, by any chance?'

In her gnarled, brown-spotted hand, she was holding the old bronze fob watch.

'Yes, it is! But I threw it in the water. How did you . . .?'

'Would you like it back?' said the woman, ignoring Eddy's confusion.

'Oh, yes please!' Eddy got to her feet and caught the watch as the woman threw it across the stream. 'Avril gave it to me.'

'She must care about you very much, giving you something as precious as that.'

'She does . . .'

The old woman lowered her hand again. Now Eddy could see her eyes: one a murky green, the other dark amber. They crinkled at her kindly. 'Well, if anything's worth hanging on for, that is.'

'Eddy!'

The shout came from up on the road. Eddy recognised the voice immediately. 'Lionel . . .?' She turned her head to look through the trees. Sure enough, her old friend was on the road, searching around the yellow Mini and calling her name.

'Another friend of yours?' said the old woman. 'You're a lucky girl.'

'Yes, I suppose I am . . .' Eddy turned back to face her and stopped.

The opposite bank was empty. The old woman was gone.

'Eddy, where are you? It's me, Lionel!'

Eddy blinked very hard to clear her eyes and scrambled to her feet. 'Lionel, I'm here!' She began to make her way up the bank, slipping on the mud in her hurry. Before she climbed up on to the road, she glanced down at the fob watch, hardly believing it was there again in her hand. As she flipped it open, she let out a gasp. The glass was still shattered, but beneath it, the second hand suddenly moved. It was still six minutes and twenty-nine seconds to three, and now the clock was ticking. 'It's not broken . . .' Eddy ran through the trees, on to the road. 'Lionel, I'm so glad you're here. I just met this woman . . . I thought it was a dream, but then the watch was mended . . .'

O'Neill stared at the wild-haired, blood-stained figure racing towards him. 'Are you all right?'

Eddy threw her arms around him and hugged him

tightly for a moment. 'I *will* be all right. But you have to take me to Leviticus, Lionel, as fast as you can. Avril will have a cure. I just know it.'

19

Red Herring

'No!' hissed Dr Wetherby, peering through his rat-head around the corner at the throng of white-coated Leviticus scientists. 'I'm not walking down there, Dr Crump! Look at all these CCTV cameras . . .'

'Raymond, get a grip. You know, I doubt anyone will even be watching the CCTV.' Avril waved a scarlet-clad arm at the silent cameras. 'When I did my Save Our Vending Machines demo last February, it was two days before anyone even noticed me on camera. Now come on.' She pulled at Dr Wetherby's arm and stepped out into the corridor. 'All we have to do is get up to Lab One and back out again.'

'Oi! You two. Fish-tail and Fatty.'

The hand that landed on Avril's shoulder was like a lead weight.

'Where's your identification badges?' said the owner of the hand, spinning Avril around to face him. It was Red Herring. He moved in front of Avril, barring the way to the Tower staircase.

'These stairs is a Restricted Area,' he said. 'And I don't see your identity badges.'

'Quite, quite. Well so sorry to have bothered you,' began Dr Wetherby, muffled behind his rat head. 'You just carry on doing the fine job that you're doing, and we'll be on our way . . .'

Avril put out a foot to trip him as he tried to turn around and hurry away.

'Oh, but we're just a couple of actors,' she said brightly, looking up at the guard and batting her eyelashes so violently that her false beard jiggled up and down in sympathy. 'We're here for Science for KidZ week. We need to rehearse in the Tower.'

The guard peered down his flattened nose at them. 'I'm just gonna check with my boss, Mother Mary.'

'No!' Avril yelped, flapping her hand in agitation. 'There's no need for that! We're only actors, aren't we?' She dug Dr Wetherby in his scaly ribs. '*Aren't we?*' she repeated.

'Oh, yes. Romeo, Romeo, and all that,' Dr Wetherby muttered.

The guard stopped, his finger still hovering over the Talk button.

'To be,' Dr Wetherby added for good measure, 'or not to be? That is the question.'

'All right then, Fish-Man. Off you go.'

'I'm a *Mer-Rat*,' snapped Dr Wetherby, before being silenced by a kick from Avril.

Red Herring raised a tattooed hand in warning. 'But if you're not back down here an hour from now, I'm calling Mother Mary for sure.'

'One hour. Absolutely.' Avril was already hopping up the first stairs.

20

One Man and His Dog

'Might I sing a humble working-man's ditty, Mr Dog,
to accompany me while I dig?'

'If you want me to bite you on the ankle,' Augustus
muttered, pacing up and down in great agitation.

'I'm but a humble working man,
my brain may not be big,
but freedom is my daring plan
– past wall, and yard, and pig!
No man, no beast, no grazing porker
will stop our flight from Mr Stalker.
A simple scheme – but what a corker!
I dig, and dig, and dig!
I dig for Mr Dog, huzzah!
I toil without a question.

For Mr Dog is such a star,
despite his poor digestion.
And though . . .'

'Bony, if you mention my digestion one more time . . .'
Then Augustus fell silent, and cocked an ear. '*Someone's coming.*'

There were footsteps outside, which stopped some distance away, and a great deal of breathless panting.

'Well done, Gormy. Now Daddy's got another treat for you.'

Augustus inhaled deeply. There was a new smell out in the yard, a smell he half-recognised. But Obadiah's pong made it impossible to identify clearly.

'He's got a sidekick!' Augustus hissed. '*Another crazed Mr Dog fan!*'

'Now, you just leave the dog to me,' said Obadiah. 'I got plans for that dog, money-making plans, but O'Neill wouldn't be happy if he knew I was ignoring his instructions.'

'Who is this O'Neill?' Bonaparte had stopped digging and pressed his ear up against the wall.

'Probably their leader,' Augustus said. 'The

Biggest Augustus Fan of all. Lord only knows the depths of *his* obsession.'

'So, you listen to me, Gormy. When I say go, you get in there and deal with the tall one. Not as much meat on him as that tasty pig, but he'll do for a bit o' fun.'

Augustus stared at Bonaparte. 'Does he mean what I think he means?'

Bonaparte huffed. 'I do believe that I am being unfavourably compared with an animal of the porcine variety.'

'You ready, Gormy?'

There was an answering whimper of excitement. Augustus' ears pricked up. 'It's a *dog*?' he said in disbelief.

'One . . . two . . .'

Bonaparte's jaw dropped in amazement as a large brown dog came hurtling into the room, teeth bared ready to tear into flesh. For a split second, he stared from the new dog to Augustus and back again, before Augustus launched himself at his look-alike with a rather startled volley of barks. Gormenghast, sleek and well-prepared for attack, flung him off like he was no more than an irritating bluebottle and went for Bonaparte.

'Run, Bony!' Augustus gurgled, managing to get in Gormenghast's way again long enough for Bonaparte to bolt for the door.

'Gormy! After him!' Obadiah tried and failed to snatch at Bonaparte's sleeve as the shrieking clone fled.

'Over my dead body!' yelled Augustus, neatly tripping up Gormenghast with his tail. The fitter dog sprawled on the floor for a moment, looking slightly dazed, but sprang to his paws with a snarl as Augustus made for the door himself.

'Oh, no you don't, doggy!' Obadiah moved quicker this time and stepped in front of Augustus, aiming a kick between his eyes. As Augustus sank to the floor, the last thing he saw was Gormenghast leaping out of the barn door to give chase to Bonaparte.

★

Wilfred, whose frantic chiselling had created an almost Wilfred-sized hole in the shed wall, heard the commotion from the yard and sprang to the window. He saw Bonaparte hurtling across the yard like a champion sprinter.

'Bony, stop!'

But the clone did not hear his advice, which was just as well. Ten seconds behind him was Gormenghast, slavering in excitement and ready for the main course after his hors d'oeuvre of pig. Then Obadiah Grimley-Stenching marched out of the barn, carrying Augustus.

'Never mind O'Neill's orders,' Wilfred heard him say. 'You're gonna make my fortune, doggy.'

Obadiah carried Augustus to an old Land Rover, put the dog inside and then clambered in himself. 'Sell him for thousands . . .'

From just behind the tractor, Wilfred caught Augustus' eye. The two of them stared at each other for a moment, then the Land Rover sped away.

Wilfred leapt up into the tractor, crossed his fingers tightly, and started the engine.

21

Puddleball

Bonaparte ran as fast as his spindly legs could carry him, not daring to cast a glance back over his shoulder. If he could just reach those crowds of people on the Green before the snarling hound caught up with him, he would be safe. He could see the Green now as he rounded the corner of the lane. 'Help!' he yelled, waving his arms so wildly above his head that his speeding legs were almost propelled off the ground. 'I beg of thee, help me!'

On the Green, the Puddleball crowd was cheering and shouting at top volume. Klaxons blared and rattles rattled, and a strange cloud of what looked like steam rose up from the middle of the Green, above the bobbing heads of the spectators.

'Will no one assist me in my dreadful plight?' gasped Bonaparte. Someone on the edge of the crowd glanced around. It was the young man who had spoken to them in the lane earlier. His eyes widened in alarm as he saw the extraordinary figure bowling at speed towards him.

'Oh, please, kind sir! As an old friend, help me!'

The young man decided that it would be far better to help himself. He stepped neatly out of Bonaparte's way before he was done an injury. Bonaparte shot straight through this new gap in the line . . .

. . . and on to the Puddleball pitch.

For a moment, Bonaparte stopped. He stared at the sight before him: a large group of burly men, all clad in green and white, had formed a chaotic pile of writhing bodies in the middle of the Green. Then he heard Gormenghast howl behind the crowd, and he ran towards the piled bodies.

A blood-stained man clawed his way out from the bottom of the pile, clutching a dark brown oval ball to his chest. One half of the crowd erupted into cheers, and Bonaparte decided that this hero must be the man to help him.

'Oh, good sir – I prithee help me. I am fleeing . . .'

'You the replacement for Puddleton Number 13?' yelled the player with a glance at Bonaparte's red jacket. 'You took your time!'

'But I am not …' gasped Bonaparte, as the man pulled him towards the middle of the pitch.

★

Several hundred yards away, bumping along the lane in the Land Rover, Augustus had just noticed that the window beside him was half-open. If he could open it a few more inches, it would be wide enough for him to leap out.

'Where are we going?' he said, pretending to be groggy from the blow to his head and edging his tail towards the window handle.

'You shut up so's I can concentrate,' snarled Obadiah.

'By all means. I'd hate to be responsible for disturbing a great mind in action,' Augustus said loudly, whilst surreptitiously winding the tip of his tail around the window handle. 'For all I know, there's a cure for cancer just bursting to get out of that brain of yours. Or a solution to world peace, perhaps. Tell me,' Augustus finished edging the window open and now used the tip of his tail to pull a length of the seatbelt towards him. 'Do *you* know the date of the Battle of the Somme?'

They were approaching the Green now, and the enormous cheering crowd coming up on their left was the final distraction that Augustus needed. He pulled the seatbelt taut with his tail.

'Watch out!' he suddenly yelled. This made Obadiah slam on the brakes, and the seatbelt catapulted Augustus out of the open window.

'Aaaaaaaaah . . .' was his only possible comment. For a glorious few seconds of flight, he sailed through the air, high above the heads of the crowd below, and above Obadiah, who had jumped out of the Land Rover. The wind was beneath the dog's floppy ears, his four legs splayed outwards as he soared to freedom . . .

. . . and then he landed in the brawny arms of a Puddleball player.

'Got it!' gasped the player, thinking he had the ball.

'Go on!' yelled the Puddleswick crowd. 'Score, score, score!'

'Now hang on just one moment . . .'

The Puddleswick player had the red mist of goal-scoring glory before his eyes, and so did not notice that his ball was talking to him. With an animal yell, he began to charge forwards.

Augustus gazed ahead in alarm. The idiot was heading directly into a pack of other players, who looked suspiciously like a bunch of escaped lunatics. And just before they barrelled into the hungry, snarling pack, Augustus' eyes met a more-than-averagely crazed pair, wide with anticipation, at the front of the pack. '*Bonaparte?*'

'Mr Dog!'

Then everything went dark. For a moment, all Augustus could see was knobbly knees and scrabbling hands, and all he could hear was a variety of colourful words which had had never heard before, until Bonaparte's beaming face loomed through the pile towards him.

'Greetings, Mr Dog! 'Tis a most unexpected pleasure.'

'What on earth's the matter with you, Bony?' Augustus curled up into a protective ball as brutish hands grabbed at him. 'What *is* this living hell?'

''Tis the glorious game of Puddleball, Mr Dog!' came Bonaparte's voice through all the surrounding grunting and groaning. 'Take *that*, sir,' he shrieked, gleefully, sticking a bony elbow into an inconveniently-placed set of ribs. 'Is't not the most marvellous fun?'

'Fun?' Augustus gasped in disbelief. 'What's the matter with y –'

A pair of hairy hands suddenly seized him and Augustus was pulled out of the claustrophobic dark into bright and freezing fresh air. It was then that he heard the familiar howl of Gormenghast, and the rasping voice of Obadiah, fighting his way through the crowd and egging his dog on to violence.

'Get 'em, Gormy! *Get 'em!*'

Out of the corner of his eye, Augustus could see the crazed dog running up and down the side of the pitch, eyes fixed on the pile of bodies, waiting for Bonaparte to emerge.

'Score, score, score . . .' urged the Puddleton fans, leaping in collective glee as their player emerged with the ball – which, if anyone had been calm enough to realise, was kicking and yelling nearly as frantically as they were.

'This is too much! Let go of me! I'm an international star-in-the-making. I won't be dog-handled in this disrespectful manner!'

Tackled from behind, the Puddleton player

suddenly hit the ground. He let go of Augustus for just long enough for a fresh pair of hands to grab him and pick him up.

"'Tis I, Mr Dog!'

'Oh, thank heavens.' Augustus swivelled in Bonaparte's tight grip to see his friend's face. 'Bony? I don't like that glint in your eye . . .'

With a war-like whoop, Bonaparte turned around and began to run in the opposite direction.

'There shall be no stopping me now, Mr Dog.' Bonaparte did not even notice that Gormenghast was on the pitch and was running at full pelt after him, along with at least half the players. The vicious dog was tangled up in their legs for a moment, nipping and snarling at them as they got in his way.

'You leave my Gormy alone!' screamed Obadiah, battling unsuccessfully through the crowd.

'Bonaparte, I command you to listen to me!' Augustus yelled. 'That dog will eat you alive. Stop this nonsense and run away from here!'

Bonaparte had not listened to a word. 'For the glory of Puddleton!' he launched himself through the air, lifted Augustus up high, and thumped him down in the freezing mud on the other side of the score line.

Silence fell, and Gormenghast stopped running. For a moment, the only noise on the Green was the dog's low growling as he awaited his moment, anticipating the kill with every globule of saliva that dripped from his jaws.

'He's done it,' someone piped up angrily from the midst of the Puddleton fans. 'He's only gone and scored an own goal.'

'Indeed.' Bonaparte hopped excitedly from foot to foot. 'My *very own* goal!'

'Not *your* own goal, you bleedin' idiot!' The Puddleton players advanced on Bonaparte with raised fists. '*An* own goal. You scored one for the opposition!'

Bonaparte blinked at them. 'So 'twas *not* for the glory of Puddleton?'

At the end of the Green, the final whistle blew.

'Puddleswick, one hundred and forty-nine points, Puddleton, one hundred and thirty-six points,' yelled the referee. 'Puddleswick win the match with an own goal scored by Substitute Number thirteen. Puddleton lose for the five hundredth year in a row.'

'*Kill him!*'

Bonaparte backed away from the pitch in alarm as

the Puddleton crowd, an unusual shade of mottled mauve above their red and white clothing, surged forward.

'Mr Dog, get up!' Bonaparte gasped, pulling at Augustus' tail. 'Thou hast made a terrible mistake.'

'*I've* made a mistake?' Spitting out mouthfuls of wet mud, Augustus slipped and slid to his paws, then stared at the small riot in front of him. 'Run, Bony, run!'

'Mr Dog, I can run no longer! I have not stopped running for nigh upon half an hour.'

'Well, that'll teach you to play Puddleball,' Augustus snapped. 'Of all the ignominious . . .'

He stopped. Bouncing along the lane ahead of them, across the other side of the Green, was the tractor.

'The kid,' said Augustus.

'The tractor,' sighed Bonaparte.

'Augustus!' Wilfred waved frantically from high up in his tractor. 'Bony! I'm coming! But I can't stop! You'll have to jump up!'

'Are you ready, Bony?' said Augustus. 'One . . . two . . .'

On three, they jumped.

Augustus landed neatly on the battered old seat, only to be thrown upwards as Bonaparte landed more heavily beside him. The dog clutched at the first thing available to him, which happened to be Wilfred's glasses. The spectacles fell to the floor, beneath the brake pedal.

'I can't see anything!' cried Wilfred, letting go of the steering wheel in his panic.

'Bony, find those glasses!' barked Augustus. 'I'll steer!'

As Bonaparte scrabbled beneath Wilfred's feet and Wilfred stared blindly about at the chaos surrounding him, Augustus grasped the steering wheel with his teeth.

'But you can't see either!' Wilfred yelled at the dog, whose head did not rise above the wheel.

'Maybe not,' Augustus let go of the wheel to say, irritably, 'but *I*, at least, have superb instincts.'

Then there was a very loud crunch.

Unguided and careering into a large clump of trees, the tractor hit a trunk head-on, and came to a sudden and dramatic halt.

'I have thy spectacles, Young Master Wilfred!' Bonaparte emerged from the tractor floor with a beam to see the crestfallen faces of Wilfred and Augustus. 'All is well again!'

'All is not w-well, Bony,' said Wilfred. 'The engine has stopped running.'

22

Lab One Again

Lab One was filled with the smell of fresh paint. The small room was a white, anonymous box. The cracked pane of glass in the tiny window had been replaced, and the old loose floorboards had been taken up, the concrete underneath scrubbed and whitewashed. It was as though the explosion from Uncle Edgar's chemistry set and the Replication Chamber had never happened.

Avril sank to the whitewashed floor. 'It used to be so cosy . . .' Her throat thickened. 'I had so many little hiding places, just in case anyone came up here and tried to pinch a jammy dodger. There was a loose floorboard just here, and an old mouse-hole in that corner. I thought that's where the Formula might be.

But there's nothing left.' She gazed about at the chilly whitewashed walls. 'How am I going to save Edna now?'

Dr Wetherby scratched the rat head he was holding under his arm. 'Can't you take her to a doctor?'

'That won't help! There's no doctor in the world who can cure the Slumber Code!' She stared helplessly out of the new windowpane, her false beard soggy with tears. 'I can't lose her.'

Dr Wetherby shuffled his mermaid tail awkwardly. 'I'm very sorry. In her own rather unruly way, Edna was a good friend to my Wilfred. Let's hope . . .'

'Don't talk about her as if she were already gone!' Avril howled. 'She's my best friend in the whole world. The *first* friend I ever had! And there's nothing I can do for her! I can't make her better just by *hoping*. I wish she was here with me now. I wish they were all here – Augustus, and Bony . . .'

Avril stopped howling. She stared down at her rucksack where she had dropped it on the floor.

'Bony,' she whispered.

'I would like to express my deepest sympathy, Dr Crump, in this your hour of sorrow. Although thanks to you I have been kidnapped; almost blown up –

twice; threatened with everything from Room 237 to drug-filled syringes; thrown out of eleventh-storey windows; dressed up as a mutating mermaid . . . Dr Crump, what *are* you doing?'

Avril had emptied the entire contents of her rucksack on to the floor and was searching through it with shaking hands. Over her shoulder flew her balaclava, a stub of crayon, the foil-wrapped sandwich and the broken top half of a Bunsen burner before she found what she was looking for.

'Raymond!' She held the pile of muffins up to him as though they were manna from heaven. 'This is it!'

'Dr Crump, might I ask how you think that some slightly grubby cakes will ease your mental torment?'

'Because they're the cure! At least, one of them is . . .' She took a tiny nibble of each before spitting the mouthful of the smallest one out. Unlike the others, which were still fresh and tasty, the small muffin was dry, hard and starting to shrivel slightly at the edges. 'This is the one that soaked up Bony's concoction!' With a beam splitting her face, she scrambled to her feet. 'Tastes absolutely foul!'

Dr Wetherby took a large step backwards. 'Extreme stress *can* bring on a sudden attack of madness . . .'

'Raymond, I'm not mad! We've got Gideon's Formula after all! Yesterday Bony made a mixture from a formula he found in my old papers from Leviticus. *I knocked it over by accident and it's in this muffin . . .*' She waved the muffin under his nose. 'So we've got it, Raymond! We've got the cure. All Edna has to do is eat it!'

'Dr Crump, I do not understand a single word you have just gibbered.'

'I'll explain it on the drive back to Chez Crump.' Avril placed the small, dry muffin into the front zip pocket of the rucksack with all the care her trembling hands would allow and ran for the door, her ermine-trimmed cloak flowing out behind her. 'Come on, Raymond! Let's get out of here. We've got to rescue Edna!'

23

Augustus' Superpowers

'Mr Dog!' Bonaparte hissed across the tractor seat at Augustus. The tractor had rolled deeper into the spinney, and was shielded from the distant village Green by thick fir trees. The roars from the Puddleball riot had ceased half an hour ago. 'Thinkest thou that Young Master Wilfred knowest what he doth do with yon engine?'

Augustus did not reply. He was sniffing the air with growing urgency and his ears were twitching uncomfortably.

'Bony, quiet! For all we know, Obadiah and Gormenghast escaped the riot. They might be looking for us!' Wilfred's face was smeared with oil and his brow was furrowed with concentration. 'Any minute now, I'll have this engine going again and we'll be on our w-way.'

'I do hope so, Young Master Wilfred.' Bonaparte sniffed. ''Twould be a boon indeed if one small thing did go well on this terrible day.'

'Come on, Bony, chin up!' Wilfred saw the clone's thin shoulders slump in the gathering afternoon gloom. 'Not everything's gone wrong. We've got transport, for starters, and we got rid of Obadiah and his horrible d-dog. I only hope Eddy's all right.'

'But Miss Eddy must have gone with dear Mr Lionel,' said Bonaparte. 'No harm can come to her with our good friend.'

'But that's just what I was trying to tell you five minutes ago, Bony,' Wilfred sighed. 'I'm not sure Lionel *is* our friend. I heard him talking to the farmer, and –'

He was interrupted by Augustus. 'Oh, stop blithering on about Lionel, will you? I would like to declare a state of national emergency.' His whole body was bristling with agitation. '*My super-powers are gone.*'

'Gone?' echoed Bonaparte.

'Gone,' repeated Augustus. A note of panic had entered his voice. 'I cannot hear your whispers. I cannot detect the customary scent of stew. And heaven only knows what's happened to my gift of healing! I am a broken dog,' he continued, slumping down on the battered seat and covering his eyes with shaking paws. 'Despite my great physical strength, my incredible sporting prowess, and my honed athlete's body, I do not respond well to being used . . .' – his voice almost failed him – '*as a Puddle Ball*.'

'Oh, Mr Dog, what have I done?' Bonaparte flung himself on the dog, only to receive a distressed nip to the knucklebones. 'I knew not that thy super-powers were so delicate a gift!'

'They weren't *delicate*!' yelled Augustus, raising his head. 'They just failed to rise to the challenge of being battered about by a pack of paunchy Puddleballers!'

'Calm down, Gus . . .'

'Not Gus!' howled the dog. '*Never* Gus!'

'Oh, Mr Dog, Mr Dog . . .' wept Bonaparte. 'I shall never forgive myself! Here . . .' – he scrabbled inside his mud-covered red jacket. 'Perhaps thou might be cheered by thy much-cherished stick.'

'*It's not my cherished stick!*'

Bonaparte pulled out the stick. It was somewhat shorter than he remembered. And then he realised why.

'Oh, what a calamity,' he said, his lower lip starting to wobble. 'Another casualty of yon terrible game of Puddleball. Thy stick is broken in two.'

Augustus stared at the two halves of his stick. 'My cherished stick . . .' he managed to say.

Bonaparte was lost for words. He simply let out a repentant howl.

'*Please*, you two, keep quiet!' Wilfred was desperate. The engine was not chugging to life as fast as he had hoped, and he could not stop worrying about Eddy.

'Quiet? At a time of national emergency?' Augustus was furious. 'Well, I like that! I should have stayed with the crazed stalker! I should have taken my chances with the mysterious O'Neill! At least *he's* a Mr Dog fan! Probably the head of the Mr Dog Worshippers' Society or something.'

'O'Neill?' Wilfred frowned, his hand hovering over the greasy fan-belt. 'I heard the farmer mention O'Neill as well. You know, I'm starting to think this O'Neill had something to do with Lionel telling the farmer to kidnap you.'

'*Lionel* told the farmer to kidnap us?' This was so astonishing that Augustus forgot his fury with Bonaparte.

'Augustus, I've been telling you that since we crashed! Didn't *you* think there was anything funny about Lionel when he showed up in Puddleton?'

'His nose, perhaps, was a little more comic than usual,' mused Bonaparte. 'And perhaps there was something amusing in his arthritic gait . . .'

'Not funny ha-ha! Funny peculiar.'

'No more so than usual,' Augustus said. 'But Lionel didn't mention this O'Neill to *us*. If he'd wanted to introduce me to head of the Mr Dog Worshippers' Society, why didn't he just ask?'

'A Society,' said Bonaparte sadly, 'that shall be no more, now that thy super-powers are so terribly compromised.'

Augustus lay down and put his paws over his eyes.

'O'Neill . . .' murmured Wilfred, returning to the tractor engine. 'Who are you . . .?'

★

The yellow Mini sped through the open iron gates of Leviticus and screeched into a vacant space.

Eddy gazed about the deserted car park, desperately searching for Avril's little green sports car.

'Do you even think Avril's still here?' she asked.

'Of course I do!' said O'Neill, giving her a colossal grin and a big thumbs-up.

Eddy blinked at him, taken aback for a moment. 'Lionel, I know you're trying to stay positive for me. But I can't see her car or anything . . .'

'Oh, Avril's a smart cookie. She'll have hidden it somewhere, ready for a swift getaway. Now,' – he waved a hand up at the Tower – 'I'm sure she's up in that little old Lab of hers working away on that cure. Shall we go and get her?'

Eddy was still uncertain, but she appreciated Lionel's relentless optimism. 'You're probably right.' As she opened her car door to get out, the fob watch, which she had been holding tightly in her left hand, slipped from her grasp and rolled underneath the car seat. 'Oh! Lionel – can you help? I've dropped Avril's watch!'

'There's no time,' O'Neill hissed across the car park, casting glances over his shoulder. 'We'll get it later, I promise. It'll still be there when we come back. Come on!'

Eddy followed him through the oak door. 'We must watch out for the security guards, Lionel,' she whispered.

'We don't need to worry about a little thing like that!' O'Neill called over his shoulder as he sprinted down the corridor in the direction of the Tower.

Eddy put on a burst of speed to catch up with him. 'It's so nice to have someone to look after me,' she said, putting her hand through his. He held on tightly as they reached the doorway to the Tower's spiral staircase.

'Let's go.'

Eddy raced up the stairs behind him. He was taking them four or five at a time, still clutching her hand.

O'Neill's face was reddening with the exertion. 'Come on! We must hurry.'

At the top of the eleventh flight, O'Neill suddenly stopped. 'Tell you what, young Eddy,' he said. 'I'll go on up to the next floor to Lab One alone, shall I? To make sure it's safe.'

Eddy smiled up at him. 'You want to see Avril for a moment by yourself, don't you?'

O'Neill turned even more red. 'Er . . . well . . .'

'No problem, Lionel. I know she'll be thrilled to see you.'

'Great!' O'Neill pulled Eddy on to the eleventh

floor corridor. 'Lab 99. You can wait in here.'

He tried the handle and the door opened.

★

Avril stopped at the top of the stairs.

'Did you hear something? On the floor below? It sounded like a door closing.'

'There must be someone there,' hissed Dr Wetherby. He jammed his rat head back on so tightly that Avril winced. 'Careful!' he beseeched Avril, as she began to tiptoe down the stairs towards the eleventh floor.

There was another noise. This time it was not a door closing, and Avril could hear it quite clearly. It was a man's voice, coming from behind a door on the floor below, and it said one word, very loudly.

'*Help!*'

She stared back up the stairs to Dr Wetherby, who was cowering and clutching the banister.

'Did you hear *that*?'

Dr Wetherby nodded his enormous rat head. 'It's a trick,' he hissed. 'Somebody knows you're a soft-hearted old nitwit, and they know you'll come if they call for help. For God's sake, woman, show some judgement for once!'

But Avril was already hurrying down the last stairs and on to the eleventh-floor corridor. Her heart was racing as she reached Lab 100, where the voice was calling from, and she put her shoulder to the hinge without wasting time seeing if it was locked.

There was a loud splintering sound that made Dr Wetherby bury his rat-head in his hands. But the noise had nothing on the yell that came from Avril's lips as she rushed through the broken door and into Lab 100.

'It's you,' she said. 'Lionel!'

24

Anagrams

'O'Neill . . . Lionel . . . Obadiah . . .' Wilfred muttered
again, as his fifth attempt to start the tractor engine in
as many minutes failed. 'O'Neill . . .'

'Chanting an incantation isn't going to bring my
powers back, you know.' Augustus was sulking.

'I'm just trying to w-work out the connection.'
Wilfred went back to the engine and peered into it
again, desperately searching for the reason why it
would not just start.

'Well, concentrate on working out how to start this
old rust-bucket instead!' said Augustus. 'Otherwise
Bossy Boots and old What's-His-Name will be on their
way back from Leviticus before we've even started.
Oh, stop wailing, Bony,' he sighed, as the clone started

a fresh round of hysterics. 'It'll be all right. My powers of healing are probably still intact.'

'Dost thou really think so, Mr Dog?'

'Well, let's see if I can start this tractor with the simple power of thought.' Augustus closed his eyes, placed his paws over the engine and began to hum.

'What's-his-name . . .' Wilfred's forehead had begun to hurt with frowning. 'Old What's-his-name . . .' Then it hit him. 'Oh!' he said, turning very white. There was a loud clatter as he dropped his spanner into the engine. 'Oh, no.'

The spanner hit the axle, and the engine roared into life.

'You see!' Augustus turned to Bonaparte, who shrieked with relief and glee. 'I've still got it! Perhaps I can heal my stick after all!'

'Augustus, you're a genius!' Wilfred scrambled up into the tractor seat with shaking legs.

'Well, I prefer to think of it as a heaven-sent gift, but I suppose there is a hefty dose of my own brilliance in there . . .'

'No, Augustus, not the tractor! You just put your finger on it!'

'Paw,' said Augustus, coldly, reaching for the two

halves of his stick with his teeth. 'I own nothing so mundane as a finger.'

Wilfred tried the accelerator and the tractor edged forward. He was trembling so hard that he could hardly co-ordinate himself, and it was so dusky that he scrabbled about to turn the tractors lights on. It was only then that he realised that there were no lights. 'We'll never get there in this darkness!'

'I have a box of matches, Young Master Wilfred,' Bonaparte volunteered, reaching into his pocket for the matches he had used in the garage late the previous night.

'That'll do us no good!' Wilfred was squinting through the gloom, barely able to see but determined not to stop. There was no time for that. 'I've worked out the connection between Lionel and O'Neill.' He steered in what he hoped was the direction of the road, pushing his glasses up his nose. 'Oh, this is hopeless! We can't go this slowly! There must be headlights *somewhere*.'

'What's the connection?' The dog stared up at Wilfred's frightened face as the boy stopped the tractor and began to hunt for a light switch once again.

'If you rearrange the letters in Lionel's name,' said Wilfred, 'what do you get?'

There was a bewildered silence.

Then Bonaparte gasped. 'Ill One!'

'Er – no, Bony, you get . . .'

'Oh, don't be silly, Bony,' said Augustus. 'I'm the fellow you want for this sort of thing.' He thought for a moment, creasing his brow, then spoke. 'Lo Line.'

'Lo Line?' echoed Wilfred. 'No, no, Augustus, you get . . .'

Augustus raised a paw. 'Oi, Nell, then,' he announced. 'Or maybe Enolil. Or Len Oil. Am I winning?'

'Augustus, it's not a game . . .'

'El Lion.'

'Brilliant, Mr Dog!'

'But that isn't what . . .'

'Noelli!' shouted Augustus furiously. 'Beat that, kid.'

'*O'Neill!*' Wilfred shouted back. 'You get O'Neill. The man we thought was Lionel was really O'Neill: Eddy's gone to Leviticus with Lionel's clone.'

There was a longer silence. Then Augustus spoke, almost to himself. 'I should have left her my stick after all . . .' Then he shook himself from his ears to his paws. 'Let's get this tractor moving!'

'But we can't see properly!'

'Bonaparte – those matches, if you please.' Augustus spoke with authority. 'I want you to light my stick.'

Bonaparte gasped. 'But Mr Dog . . .'

'No, Bony, it's an order. We have to save Eddy. Now, get this tractor rolling, kid. Let there be light!'

25

The Fastest Kangaroo

Lab 99 was empty apart from the large, black leather chair beside the window in the curved wall.

'Eddy, why don't you have a seat, while I go up to Lab One. You look exhausted.' O'Neill motioned her towards the large leather chair.

'I'm fine.' Eddy was exhausted, but she scrunched up her left hand and stuffed it into her pocket before the new number could imprint itself on to her mind.

2

'No, really, Eddy, you must be very tired.' O'Neill began to draw her towards the chair. 'You must save your energy.'

Eddy had to admit that the chair did look awfully comfortable, and all the running up stairs had left her rather shaky in the legs. 'Well . . .'

There was a sudden crash from out in the corridor, like a nearby door being busted open.

'What was that?' said Eddy.

'Don't you worry. Just sit down while I go and check.'

Eddy smiled up at him. 'Thank you, Lionel. I don't know what I'd do without you.'

She sat down in the soft leather seat, stretched her arms out on the padded arm-rests, and leaned her head back.

Suddenly, two metal clasps tightened around her wrists, and the chair tilted backwards.

Eddy gasped.

'Lionel! What just happened?'

O'Neill was checking the clasps on her wrists. It took a moment for Eddy to realise that he was not trying to undo them.

'Nice and secure . . .' he muttered, as the chair tilted again, so that Eddy was lying horizontally, as if in a dentist's chair. She could see nothing but the bright whiteness of the ceiling above her, and even turning her head was no use. Lionel was at her feet, and out of her view.

'Lionel,' she said again, trying to keep the tremor out of her voice. 'Lionel . . .?'

But there was no reply.

Then Eddy heard the door open and shut, and a new set of light, elegant footsteps walk into the room. She turned her head to see who they belonged to.

★

'Lionel!' Avril rushed through the broken door of Lab 100. Lionel was tied around his ankles and wrists with ropes, and a gag that had been around his mouth hung loosely about his neck, chewed in half by his own desperate teeth.

'My dearest!' Lionel's hair was wild and his clothes shambolic. 'You're a sight for sore eyes! That Santa costume looks simply perfect on you.'

'Quiet!' Dr Wetherby hissed, leaping into the lab so fast that his rat-head toppled off. He was sweating. 'I just heard someone coming up the stairs . . .'

Avril went to the doorframe and peered out an inch into the corridor. When she pulled back, she was sweating as much as Dr Wetherby. 'It's Gideon,' she mouthed. 'He's just gone into Lab 99.'

'*Now* how do we get out of here?' Dr Wetherby looked as if he might be sick. 'We never should have stopped!'

'Then we'd have run into him on the stairs.' Avril was fumbling with the ropes around Lionel's wrists, succeeding in tearing the rope in two on her second attempt.

'So *strong*,' breathed Lionel.

'Lionel, who did this to you?' Avril moved on to the ropes around his ankles, but here the knots were tighter and the rope would not tear.

'Blut's thugs came to my house last night, looking for something. I fought them tooth and nail,' he added, proudly, 'but there were two of them. I never stood a chance. When I came round, Blut was pulling out some of my hair . . .' Lionel gestured towards the battered but repaired Replication Chamber on the workbench. 'I think he's cloned me, Avril.'

'He cloned *you*?' The colour drained from Avril's face beneath her false beard and she stopped fumbling with the knots. 'Oh! He must have sent a clone to trap Edna! He seemed interested in her before. But why?'

Lionel stared at her. 'We have to find her first!'

'We must hurry!' Avril stared at the tight, complicated knots around Lionel's ankles. 'Oh dear . . .'

'I can hop to freedom!' Lionel announced. 'With you by my side, I will have the speed of the fastest kangaroo . . .'

He took a large leap forward and fell flat on his face.

'We'll carry you, Lionel,' Avril decided. 'There'll be time to untie you once we're in the car.' She picked up Lionel's bound feet and began to haul him towards the doorway. 'Raymond, I can't do this alone, you know.'

'But . . . Blut . . .' Incoherent, Dr Wetherby waved his arms.

'We'll just have to be quiet. But if we don't get past him now, we never will. Now, put on that rat-head and stop arguing. All we have to do is get out of the Tower. Then we're home free . . .'

26

Welcome to the Tower

'Welcome to the Tower.' Gideon closed the door behind him, and turned the key in the lock before moving towards Eddy. He dropped the key into his top pocket and smiled. The skin on his face stretched, showing the outline of his skull. 'I won't ask how you are. All I need to know . . .' he took a step forward, 'is how long you have left.'

'What do you want?' Eddy managed to say, staring straight up at him. 'Why am I here?'

'To save my life.'

Eddy was startled. 'To save your life?' she echoed. 'But how?'

'We will get along much better,' Gideon was walking towards her, 'if you answer my questions

208

instead of asking your own. Now, once again – *how long do you have left?*'

Eddy stared into his ocean-green eyes. They seemed brighter and clearer than ever in his tightly-stretched, ashen face. She held up her left hand as far as she could, where the number throbbed like a swollen vein.

2

Then, as both of them stared at it, the number changed.

1

'There,' Eddy said very quietly. 'That's all.'

'One hour . . .' Gideon's mouth twitched, and he stuffed his own left hand in his pocket. 'We have an hour. That should be just long enough . . . You can leave us now,' he said, sharply, to O'Neill. 'Go and find Sedukta. I am sure she will take very good care of you.'

Eddy heard the door close behind the clone as he scurried away.

'Long enough for what?' she could feel her fear rising again. 'What's going to happen to me?'

'Silence, mutant!' Gideon's eyes flashed like a wild animal's. 'I said, no questions.'

Eddy took a deep gulp of air. 'My name is not

mutant,' she said. 'It is Eddy. And if you want me to save your life, I think the very least you can do is answer my questions.' She looked up at him, feeling his grip on her hand loosen. 'Don't you?'

Gideon took a step backwards. He turned away for a moment and picked over some items on top of the lab bench – a row of sharp syringes, a stethoscope, some cotton wool and a small bowl of water.

He held up his own left hand. 'As you can see, the countdown has begun.'

Sure enough, a number glowed out from beneath his skin.

1

'You've got the Slumber Code too?' Eddy's mouth fell open.

'It was not intentional, I can assure you.' He lifted one of the syringes. 'Inside one of these syringes, I hope, lies the cure to the Slumber Code. As I have not found the exact Formula, I need to test my various attempts on a fellow sufferer.'

Eddy had begun to shake all over, but she tried very hard to remain calm, so that she could think.

'Will it hurt me?'

'Oh, not in small doses. It would be foolish of me

to harm you before I discover the correct serum, wouldn't it, mu –' He stopped, and placed a cold hand on her arm. '*Eddy.*'

The sound of her name coming from Gideon's lips for the first time made Eddy jolt.

'And will the right one *cure* me?' she whispered.

'Well, naturally. The right serum is foolproof. A certain cure.' He released the lock on her left arm, then turned away from her for a moment. Busying himself with cotton wool, he spoke again, but in a whisper. 'Of course, the incorrect dosage could be fatal. A chance I could not possibly take on myself.'

Eddy could not even hear what he said, and did not care, for relief was flooding though her. 'A certain cure,' she repeated. As Gideon turned back to face her, she held up her left arm towards him, forearm stretched out. 'Go on,' she said. 'Let's see if we can help each other.'

Gideon stared at her for a moment. Then he found his voice. 'Nothing could make me happier.' He raised the syringe and, smiling, moved towards her. 'Keep that arm right where it is, Eddy. We are about to begin.'

27

The Mini, the Motorbike and the Tractor

'If you think I'm carrying this lummock down eleven flights of stairs,' hissed Dr Wetherby as, like stretcher-bearers, he and Avril struggled down the staircase, 'you can think again.'

'Oh, come on, Raymond! You can do this.' Avril's face matched the scarlet of her cloak. 'What do you do all that aerobics for?'

'I do not do *aerobics*,' huffed Dr Wetherby, furiously. 'I do High-Impact Cardiovascular Extreme Strength and Fitness Training. With the occasional star-jump.'

'Avril, my dearest, please allow me to hop – or I can slide down the banisters!' Lionel gazed adoringly but anxiously at Avril's rear view. 'I don't want you to strain anything.'

'Don't worry, Lionel.' Avril turned her head to give Dr Wetherby a look. 'I won't strain myself. Besides, Raymond can't go anywhere fast in that mermaid tail. We'll just take it nice and steady. Better slow and sure than . . .'

'Stop! You stop right where you are! Don't move another muscle or I'll call Security!'

Santa Claus, the Mer-Rat and Lionel looked up. A familiar face was leaning over the banisters from eleven floors up.

'Heavens above,' said Lionel faintly. 'It's me.'

Dr Wetherby, too terrified to correct Lionel's grammar, gave Avril such a shove in the back of the legs with his half of Lionel that she almost toppled down to the next floor.

'For pity's sake, woman! Run!'

Hardly hearing O'Neill's furious yells and threats, the three began to hurry down the stairs, Avril running as fast as she could and Dr Wetherby half-hopping, half-stumbling in his mermaid tail.

'He's gaining on us!' gasped Lionel, the only one with a clear view of the clone's progress. 'I always knew I was a fast runner!'

'Then it's a pity we're carrying you and not Dr

Crump!' Dr Wetherby had got the hang of running in his tail but now his rat head was almost falling off. He clutched it with one hand. 'Will you get a move on, woman! Even *I* can go faster than this.'

Avril was too out of breath to reply, and her arms were starting to pull painfully at the shoulder sockets. The three hit the bottom of the stairs with only three floors separating them from O'Neill, and were through the Tower door as fast as they could stumble. But there was a surprise waiting in the corridor. It was Red Herring, and he was waving his radio.

'Hey! You actors! You been gone too long,' he said, starting to approach them. 'You stop right where you are. Mother Mary's on her way.'

But Avril was not about to stop.

'Is that a dagger I see before me?' she boomed, waving a throbbing arm at Red Herring.

Red Herring spun round in alarm, almost dropping his radio. 'Where?'

Seizing the opportunity, the trio bowled past him, Dr Wetherby sticking his leg out at the last minute, to send the guard tumbling to the ground as he tried to grab them.

'Where's your clone?' Avril panted.

Lionel craned his jolting neck to see O'Neill leap Red Herring in one neat bound, and carry on after them, closing the gap even more.

'Wow – I can long-jump too,' he marvelled, before calling up to Avril in unconvincing tones: 'Not close at all, Avril! We're home free, just like you said!'

Avril reached out to yank the huge oak door open. 'Run for my car – it's just outside the gates . . .' Then she spotted Lionel's little yellow Mini, the only car in the empty car park besides the row of huge silver motorbikes at the far end. 'Even better! Come on, boys!'

'Stop!' O'Neill's voice was even closer now, only a few feet behind Dr Wetherby. 'You'll never get out of here . . .'

'That's what *you* think,' called Avril. 'Raymond, take the weight!'

'What weight?' asked Dr Wetherby in alarm.

He soon got his answer, as Avril heaved her portion of Lionel towards him.

'Aaaaaahhh!' Dr Wetherby and Lionel were as surprised as each other as they were forced into a reluctant bear-hug. Avril had turned and was heading for O'Neill.

'Get in the car!' she yelled at them over her shoulder, before putting the same shoulder down to charge at the clone. 'Start the engine!'

The shoulder-charge was hefty enough to bring O'Neill to the ground. Dr Wetherby slung Lionel into the back seat of the Mini before hopping into the front.

★ ★ ★

At the end of the driveway, approaching the gates of Leviticus in the chugging tractor with its blazing torch at the head, Wilfred could see some activity in the middle of the car park.

'Put the torch out!' he said, switching the engine off and using the heavy vehicle's momentum to roll as silently as possible through the gates. 'Get down and stay quiet!' he told Augustus and Bonaparte, who had smothered what was left of the flaming stick with his hat.

Praying that they were not detected, he reached up from his crouched position to steer the darkened tractor away from the centre of the car park.

* * *

'The keys are in the ignition!' Dr Wetherby almost sobbed with relief, starting the engine just as Avril leapt in beside him.

'Go, go go!' she hollered from under her beard. Then a black-and-silver motorbike roared across the car park, carrying Sedukta, with a terrified Red Herring at the handlebars.

'Raymond, put your foot down!' shrieked Avril.

'But look, woman – the gates have started to close!'

'Raymond,' Avril said. 'Please. Hit that gas.'

Dr Wetherby took a very deep breath, said a very rude word, and did as he was told.

With only one sharp swerve to avoid hitting the enormous tractor-shaped vehicle that had suddenly rolled out of nowhere, dark, silent, and apparently without a driver, the little yellow Mini shot at incredible speed through the closing gates with only inches to spare.

A few critical metres behind, however, the huge silver motorbike did not fare as well. Red Herring panicked at the last second as the tractor shape loomed out of the darkness. He braked, and crunched hard

217

into the iron railings just as they shut in front of him. The last thing Sedukta saw before everything went black was the rear view of the speeding Mini, hurtling down the driveway with a distinct air of victory.

'We did it! *You* did it, Raymond!' Avril punched the air, thought about kissing Dr Wetherby on the cheek, then decided against it. 'I never thought you had it in you!'

'Nor did I,' Dr Wetherby said faintly. Then he glanced down at the speedometer and slammed on the brakes, slowing down to a near-crawl. 'That was completely illegal,' he gasped. 'Dr Crump, you should never have encouraged me to break the law like that!'

'Isn't she wonderful?' said Lionel from the back seat.

'Lionel, we must get you out of those ropes!' Avril opened the glove compartment and rummaged through it. 'We just need something to cut them with. This'll do!' she exclaimed, as a grubby old penknife tumbled out. Reaching forward to grasp the knife, she noticed something shiny on the floor beside it. As she picked it up and felt the familiar weight in her hand, she let out a horrified cry. 'It's Uncle Edgar's watch! Turn around, Raymond! We have to break into

Leviticus! They've got Edna.'

'Break in *again*?' Dr Wetherby could not believe his ears. 'But the gates!'

'This time,' said Avril, 'we're going in through my secret tunnel.'

28

The Control Centre

'Wow. That was a near miss.' Augustus stared down from the tractor at the crashed motorbike and the mangled portion of railing.

'For us,' said Wilfred, shakily. 'Not for them.' He clambered off the tractor and hurried over to the motorbike, then gasped as he recognised one of the riders. 'It's Sedukta! I think we'd better not disturb her,' he said, heading swiftly back to the tractor.

Augustus was in a bad mood. 'Well. I never thought I'd see *this* place again.'

'I've never been here before. D-dad never lets me come to work with him.'

Augustus gazed at Wilfred as the three began to head up the steps to the oak door. 'You mean you don't know the way around?'

'Er – no.' Wilfred said. 'But it'll be a challenge.'

'Oh,' said Augustus. 'Well, there's nothing I love more than a challenge.'

'Thy stick, Mr Dog,' said Bonaparte helpfully. 'That was a thing that thou did'st love more than a challenge.'

'Don't mention my stick, Bony!' snapped Augustus as they followed Wilfred through the door. 'That stick is dead to me. Now, I'd like to be carried, please. We don't know who's been walking on this floor. Bony, you shall be the official Mr Dog Bearer this time.'

Bonaparte could hardly speak as he scooped Augustus into his arms. 'And after all I did to harm thee!' he choked. 'Thou art most magnanimous!'

Augustus shifted, uncertain if this was a good thing or not. 'Well, you're not out of the woods yet, Bony.'

'Oh, but I am, Mr Dog.' Bonaparte gestured about the darkened lobby. 'I am in Leviticus Laboratories, and no longer in yon woods. 'Tis a most strange and creepy place in the dead of night,' he added in a whisper.

'This place is strange and creepy at any time of day,' Augustus said. 'No wonder his dad fits in so well here.'

But Wilfred was not listening. Uncertain of whether to turn left or right down the main corridor before them, he had just spotted the glimmerings of a torch-light around a corner at one end. He froze.

'There's someone there!'

'Who is't?' hissed Bonaparte.

'I don't know . . .'

'*I'd* be able to tell,' huffed Augustus, 'if I still had my super-powers.'

Wilfred strained his own ears, and heard the sound of two sets of heavy footsteps and the crackling of short-distance radios. The torch-light wobbled, then a voice spoke. It carried clearly down the empty corridor, so that even Augustus, with his compromised ears, could hear well enough.

'You hear all that noise out in the car park?'

'Couldn't miss it. Let's go and check it out.'

'Quick! Hide!' As the guards hurried towards the lobby, Wilfred darted for the nearest door. It read CONTROL CENTRE – AUTHORISED PERSONNEL ONLY. Luckily, it opened, and Wilfred pulled a shaking Bonaparte through and shut the door tightly.

'*Television*,' breathed Augustus.

The Control Centre was filled with television screens. There were nearly twenty of them, each flickering in black and white from one image to another as they worked their way around the cameras in each room of Leviticus.

'Closed-circuit television!' Wilfred almost whooped. 'We can look at every room in this place! We'll find Eddy much quicker that way.' Wilfred hurried for the console.

''Tis a most amazing magick.' Bonaparte could not take his eyes off the rows of screens. 'Yon television set at Lady Avril's was marvel enough – but *this*,' he breathed, 'this is beyond comprehension.'

'*Television*,' Augustus said again.

Wilfred sat at the console, tapping away furiously on the keyboard to work out how to flick through each room as fast as possible. 'Got it!' he said. 'This should go much faster now. Watch those screens on the left, Bony – and you watch the ones on the right, Augustus. I'll concentrate on the ones in the middle. If you see anything, shout out, all right?'

'OUT!' yelled Bonaparte, rehearsing.

'Now concentrate, everyone.' The screens began to flicker even more rapidly through the labs, a new image popping up on to each screen every few seconds.

'Out!' yelled Bonaparte excitedly, clutching Wilfred's shoulder.

'What, Bony, what did you see?'

'I know not precisely, Young Master Wilfred.' Bonaparte peered at his screen. 'But it doth look to me very much like a chair and . . . a window . . . and – yes, I do believe it is true – a small plant in a pot!'

'Bony, you're only supposed to shout if you see something *significant*.'

Bonaparte blinked. 'A *large* plant in a pot, perhaps?'

'No, Bony! No plants in pots! *Eddy*. Eddy's what we're looking for.'

'Ah,' Bonaparte nodded. Then his forehead creased in a concerned frown. 'But what if Miss Eddy doth *hide behind* a plant pot?'

Wilfred's mouth hung open.

'Fear not, Young Master Wilfred.' Bonaparte's attention was renewed. 'My brain is now alert!'

The light in the small room flickered like a strobe as the screens jumped from one lab to the next.

'Nought . . . nought . . . nought . . .' Bonaparte kept up a constant stream.

'Anything on your side, Augustus?'

'No,' said the dog. 'But my eyes are still quicker than anybody else's, so no doubt I will be the first to spot anything. You can even speed it up if you want,' he added, carelessly. 'Nothing important gets by me.'

'Indeed, Mr Dog! Thou art a super-being of great discernment, with the quickest of wits. Why, if thou had'st judged there to be a threat from those three extremely suspicious, heavily disguised figures breaking in from an underground lair, thou would'st have informed us in the blink of an eye.'

Augustus blinked an eye. 'What?' he said.

'What?' gasped Wilfred. 'What d-did you see, Bony?'

'Oh, Young Master Wilfred, fret not! Mr Dog did not even think it worthy of the briefest of mentions, didst thou, Mr Dog?'

'Er . . .'

Wilfred was at the keyboard, tracking back through the most recent images until he found what Bonaparte had just seen. Sure enough, three figures, fuzzy on the black-and-white screen, were helping each other out of a hole in the floor of one of the labs. One appeared to have a fish's tail and a rat's head, and was dressed in a white vest, while another looked like a rather short

Santa Claus. Even without their strange appearance, they looked furtive, with hunched shoulders, and they were running on tiptoe.

Even more significantly, they were running on tiptoe out of the lab and into the main corridor.

'They're coming this w-way!'

Bonaparte darted for the door.

'There is no lock!' he gasped.

'Hide,' said Wilfred. 'We have to hide.'

Augustus was already hiding underneath the console desk, and Bonaparte was frantically searching for a pot plant to hide behind.

'They're still coming in this direction,' Wilfred hissed, staring up at the TV screen from the floor. 'I can see them . . .' he suddenly inhaled deeply, and wrinkled his nose in disgust. 'And I think I can *smell* them . . . it's like a sewer or something!'

'I can't smell *anything*,' Augustus said mournfully. 'Oh, Mr Dog! Again, forgive me!'

'Quiet now!' Wilfred hissed.

'What if they don't go past us?' Augustus whispered.

'Then w-we'll just have to attack them. Brute force,' said Wilfred, sounding a lot more confident than he felt.

'I'm not attacking them! Not that monster of the deep! I have *standards*, you know.'

'Such a foul creature,' whimpered Bonaparte. 'So deformed, so disfigured . . .'

'They must be some of Professor Blut's experimental clones.' Wilfred could hear the six footsteps now. Together, Wilfred, Augustus and Bonaparte held their breath. All eyes were focussed on the screen . . .

. . . but the three figures went past the lobby and continued along the corridor on the other side, towards the West Tower.

29

The Last Syringe

Gideon hardly breathed as he watched Eddy. His pen was poised above his clipboard, his entire body frozen. Five serums had been injected into her arm. There was only one left.

'Do you feel *anything*?'

Eddy stared up at him. 'No. Nothing.'

Hands shaking, Gideon reached for the last syringe.

'Will this one work?' Eddy tried to meet his eyes. Their green glow was fading now, and he was struggling to keep them open. She knew what he was feeling. The tidal wave of exhaustion that was crashing through her own body was proving powerless to resist. 'I want to sleep,' she said.

'No! Don't give into it now. You want to be cured, don't you?' Gideon managed to hold the final syringe steady over her arm.

'Yes . . .'

'Of course you do. You know what's best for you.' He drew back the syringe and, with shaking hands, pressed the needle down. 'After all,' he managed to say, 'great intelligence is in your genes.'

'You mean Shakespeare,' Eddy murmured, waiting for the serum to take any effect, 'and all those people?'

'Yes,' Gideon said softly. 'All those people.' His green eyes were fixed on her odd ones. 'If this doesn't work,' he said, 'we are finished.'

But Eddy did not reply. She closed her eyes, slipping away towards the final sleep . . .

*

'I beg of thee, Young Master Wilfred, what shall we do?'

Wilfred could feel the sweat trickling down his spine, making a pool at the base of his back.

'I d-don't know yet.' He stared at the CCTV monitors. The three figures were nowhere to be seen, and nor was Eddy. 'They've just vanished. They could be anywhere.'

'Well, we can't just sit round here!' Augustus said. 'They might not be dangerous mutant clones anyway. They might just be members of some weird Leviticus Fancy Dress Society. Probably your dad in disguise,' he added witheringly, but his eyes were still wide with tension.

'Augustus! What did you just say?'

Augustus' eyes blinked through the darkness. 'Have I said something unwittingly brilliant again?'

'Without a doubt, Mr Dog!'

'You said *round*,' interrupted Wilfred. 'And look! Look at all these labs on the screen!'

Augustus and Bonaparte stared dutifully at the TV screens.

'Well, *I* know exactly what you're getting at, of course,' said Augustus. 'But poor old Bony here is rather slower on the uptake . . .'

'None of these rooms is *round*,' Wilfred said, forgetting to keep his voice to a whisper. 'And what's the first thing you notice about Leviticus?'

'Personally, the first thing I notice are the pungent pongs and the general air of rank incompetence,' said

Augustus. 'But I can't speak for the less sensitive members of our gathering.'

'Yon tower!' Bonaparte suddenly gasped. 'I did notice yon tall, round tower!'

'Precisely, Bony – yon tall, *round* tower. And none of the rooms we've seen on these screens is round. They've all got four normal w-walls, at right-angles. They've not got a curved outside wall, like they would have in a tower. You know what that means?'

Bonaparte clapped his hands and did his excitable dance of glee. 'Why, Young Master Wilfred, indeed I do! It doth clearly mean that an evil spirit is present within Leviticus Laboratories, a shape-shifting ghoul who can alter the very dimensions of time and space with a most malign intent, to convince us that a room is round when really it is square!'

There was silence for a moment.

'Er – not quite, Bony. I just meant that the CCTV isn't showing us any of the Tower labs. And that's where those people – clones, rats, whatever they w-were – must have gone. And that's why we haven't seen Eddy. She's *in the Tower*! Let's go!'

30

Anyone Care for Muffin?

'Now, let's discuss the plan,' Avril said breathlessly, as she stood with Lionel and Dr Wetherby at the bottom of the Tower stairway, her Santa cloak dripping in a fresh coat of slime from the secret tunnel.

'We could always try abseiling,' said Dr Wetherby, his voice thick with sarcasm. 'I hear the view of the fast-approaching concrete from the eleventh floor is a real treat.'

'Ignore old Whinger here,' said Lionel. 'Dear Avril, let me accost Blut, and you can take Eddy safely away.'

'No, Lionel. I don't want you to get hurt.'

Lionel looked crushed. 'Blut can't hurt me!' he said, pushing out his chest so far that he winced as his back jarred.

'I know, Lionel,' Avril patted his arm, 'but we have to be sensible. We'll need to make a fast getaway. Do you think you can work out how to open the gates? It'll slow us down too much to get out through the secret tunnel.'

Lionel frowned. 'During my investigations of Leviticus, I saw a floor-plan . . . I think I can remember where the Control Centre is.'

'Excellent! You go and get those gates open, Lionel, and have the Mini waiting for us. Raymond, I need you to keep watch here on the stairs. If Security come along, alert me as fast as possible – and *try* to do a better job than you did last time.'

'I hooted my heart out!' snapped Dr Wetherby. 'It is not *my* fault that you can't tell the distinctive call of the Great Horned Owl.'

Avril ignored him. 'Right. Are we all ready?'

'But Avril – what are *you* going to do?' Lionel reached out a hand but she was already springing up the stairs.

'I,' declared Avril, 'am going to get Edna.'

She blew him a kiss and began to thud on upwards.

Lionel and Dr Wetherby eyed each other with dislike for a moment, then Lionel turned to go back through the Tower door.

'Well,' he said. 'Good luck.'

Dr Wetherby nodded, and concentrated on the staircase.

★

'Someone's coming!' Wilfred skidded to a halt, reaching out to drag Bonaparte into the shadows with him. But Augustus was too far ahead to run back to them, and couldn't stop in time . . .

Lionel never knew what he fell over. The dog was under his feet before he had even seen him, and as he hit the floor, he lay completely dazed.

'Hey! You two! Look who I just apprehended!' Recovering from an accidental kick in the nose from Lionel's flailing feet, Augustus let out a furious volley of barks. 'Thought you could pretend to be Lionel, did you, O'Neill? Thought you could fool the great Mr Dog?'

'O'Neill?' Wilfred ran up and stared at Lionel, who had bashed his head painfully and was blinking to clear his blurred vision.

'*Wilfred* . . .?' Lionel managed to utter, but his

head was spinning. He closed his eyes and let his head fall back to the floor.

Wilfred reached down to shake him awake, but it was useless. 'What have you d-done with Eddy?'

Augustus thought fast. 'Exactly! *Eddy's* the one in danger here. And thanks to my quick thinking and bravery, I have foiled O'Neill's dastardly plans.' He glanced down at the slumped Lionel. 'We'll get nothing out of him. Come on, kid, let's get into that Tower. Bony, someone needs to guard old Doppelganger.'

'Yes, Bony,' agreed Wilfred. 'You stay here and guard O'Neill.'

'Alone?' Bonaparte stared at them and began to shake with terror. 'But I am afeard of him!'

'We're all afeard, Bony,' said Wilfred, 'but we d-don't have much time left to save Eddy.'

Bonaparte gulped. 'Then I shall do what I must.'

'Tie him up with his shoelaces,' Augustus called over his shoulder, already running towards the Tower doorway. 'We'll be back before he even stirs.'

★

Avril's strange boom-and-squeak voice meant that she

had never been talented at impersonating people. But, standing outside Lab 99, she was not about to let this put her off. If she could *feel* as tall and elegant as Sedukta, despite her Santa outfit, then maybe she would sound like her for just a moment.

'Oh, Professor . . .'

A little coy and high-pitched, perhaps, but near enough.

'It is me . . . er – I mean, it is I, Sedukta.' Avril braced herself, ready to run at the door the moment it opened. 'I've brought you that . . . that thing!'

There was silence for a moment. Then Gideon's weak voice floated out from the laboratory.

'I did not ask for anything, Sedukta. Go away.'

'No, no, not *any*thing. *That* thing. You know, the thing you really wanted . . . er . . . for the experimentation process . . .?' Avril crossed her fingers and at least nine of her toes.

'My orders were to be left alone!' Gideon opened the door. 'I do not expect . . . Dr Crump!'

He tried to slam the door, but he was too weak. Avril darted in, then stopped in horror as she saw Eddy shackled to the chair by the window.

'Edna! What have you done to her?'

Avril made a move towards Eddy but she was pushed to the floor by Gideon, summoning all the strength he had left.

'Avril . . . it's you . . . he's just trying . . . to cure me . . .' Eddy managed to open her eyes for a moment and turned her head.

'To *cure* you?' Avril gasped, just as Gideon gave her a sharp kick, rolling her towards the far wall. The fob watch that she had brought with her rolled out of her pocket. She ignored the pain and staggered to her feet, reaching into the rucksack for the muffin. 'Edna, no. He only wants to harm you . . . And *I've got the cure!*'

Gideon's head snapped back, almost as if he had been punched in the throat.

'Avril . . .?' Eddy blinked, but could not clear the fog from her eyes. 'Cure . . .?'

'This muffin. It's filled with the serum.' Avril moved towards Eddy with the dried-up muffin. But Gideon blocked her way again.

'Give it to *me* . . .' Gideon tried to snatch her arm, but Avril moved too fast. She got around him, her own arms outstretched to give the muffin to Eddy before it was too late . . .

And then she tripped over the hem of her Santa
Claus cloak outfit, and crashed to the floor.

The small, hard muffin broke into pieces.

31

Two Cases of Mistaken Identity

Bonaparte stood some distance away from his captive, too nervous to approach him even to tie him up with his shoelaces, as Augustus had instructed.

'Such evil,' he murmured fearfully, looking down at the man he presumed to be O'Neill, still dazed on the floor after his encounter with a flying Augustus. 'I see now how different thou art from my dear, true friend, Mr Lionel.'

'Bony . . .?' Lionel opened his bleary eyes at the sound of his name. 'Is that you?'

'Bony?' Suddenly, there came a shout from down the corridor. 'Is that you?' A figure was running towards them from the direction of the lobby, waving its arms wildly. It was O'Neill.

'Oh, Mr Lionel!' Bonaparte shrieked in relief and launched himself towards O'Neill. 'I thank heaven that I am no longer alone with this bad man!'

'Bad man?' repeated Lionel, struggling to get up from the cold, hard lino. 'Bony, what are you . . .' He raised a shaking hand to point at O'Neill. '*You*,' he said. 'My clone!'

'Don't listen to him, Bony,' said O'Neill hastily, skidding to a halt and giving Lionel a shove to the ground again. 'He'll poison your mind against me.'

But now Bonaparte was hesitating. He took a step away from O'Neill, then peered down at Lionel once more. 'Thou dost have a most malevolent countenance . . . but now that I look at it,' – he stared back up at O'Neill – 'so doth he . . .'

'Steady on!' Lionel was indignant as he struggled to his feet again. 'It's exactly the same countenance I had the last time I saw you. Now, come on, Bony, be sensible and listen to me. *He's* the evil clone.'

'No I'm not! He is!'

'No *I'm* not! *He* is . . .'

All three stared at each other for a long moment. Then Bonaparte managed to speak. 'Thou art identical,' he whispered, pressing his back against the wall in terror, as far from the two Lionels as he could go. 'And I confess, I know not which of thee is which . . .'

*

'Can you hear anything yet, Augustus?' Wilfred ran to the West Tower door, where the dog was waiting, and pulled it open for him. 'We need to know which floor Eddy's being held on.'

'No!' Augustus shook his head furiously. A shower of mud flew into the air. 'Will you get it into your thick skull, kid? I've lost my . . . Oh!' The dog stopped, and pricked up his ears. 'I *can* hear something . . .'

'Augustus – you must have had mud blocking your ears!' Wilfred was covered with a layer of it now himself. He blew it out of his eyes. 'That Puddleball pitch was incredibly muddy . . . and Bony *did* dump you right in it.'

Augustus was too thrilled at the return of his supersonic hearing to tell Wilfred not to mention that indignity. He was shaking his whole body now, getting every last crumb of dried mud out of his ears and nose.

'I can hear everything again!' Augustus bounded for the stairs. 'Up here, for starters. It sounds like . . . it's like an owl hooting . . .'

The dog raced up four floors, followed as fast as he could by Wilfred, who rounded the corner of the stairs to see the dog standing, stock-still, all the hairs on his back standing up.

'It's not an owl – it's the Rat-Fish!'

'Who said that?' The Mer-Rat spun around to face them, mid-hoot.

'It talks too,' said Augustus. 'How weird is *that*?'

'Run at it, Gus!' yelled Wilfred, sprinting to catch up and clenching his fists in readiness. 'We have to get past it!'

'*Wilfred Wetherby?*' The Mer-Rat clutched the banisters in shock just as the dog hurtled for his ankles. 'Get off me! Get off!'

'Augustus, stop!' Wilfred could see the terror in the familiar eyes underneath the rat's head. 'It's . . . my dad!'

Augustus turned, mid-snap. 'I realised that six bites ago. What makes you think I *want* to stop?'

'Wilfred, please! Call the dog off!' Dr Wetherby was whimpering. 'Throw him a biscuit or something.'

242

'What *is* this mistaken belief that dogs like biscuits? *Pizza*,' Augustus said, very loudly and clearly, as Dr Wetherby collapsed in a shaking heap. '*Minus the olives*.'

'D-dad – what are you *d-doing* here?' Wilfred rushed forward and pulled at the rat head.

'No! Leave that! I mustn't be caught on camera!'

'But there's no CCTV in the Tower, D-dad. D-didn't you know?'

Dr Wetherby stared down his rat nose at his son. 'Wilfred Wellington Wetherby, you'd better start explaining what you are doing here – *long* past your bedtime, I might add – and you'd better start now!'

Wilfred looked down at his feet. 'No,' he said.

'I . . . I *beg* your pardon?'

'D-dad, I can't explain w-what I'm doing here. I haven't got time now.' Wilfred looked desperately up the stairs. 'I have to rescue Eddy.'

Not looking back, he took the steps three at a time, with Augustus bounding along behind him.

32

The Cure

'No!'

With frantic sweeping motions, Avril struggled to scoop a heap of dried-up muffin crumbs into her cupped hands.

'Edna – hurry! Eat these.'

With more finesse and speed than she had ever managed in her life, Avril reached Eddy, lifted her lolling head and forced bits of the broken muffin into her mouth. The number on her trapped left hand was almost pulsating now, swollen and tinged with purple, like an ugly bruise.

'Eat it, Edna! Please eat it!' Avril saw Eddy's mouth begin to move, crunching the morsels of muffin. 'That's it, Ed . . .' Just then, Gideon managed to grasp Avril's ankle. She was pulled backwards, and then to the floor.

'Give me . . . some . . .'

Avril could hear the desperation in his voice.

'But there's none left,' she managed to say. Despite herself, she could feel the first stirrings of pity for Gideon. But she forced herself to look towards Eddy again.

Eddy's whole body had begun to judder. From the top of her head all the way down to her toes, she seemed to be possessed by some sort of electrical energy.

'What's happening?' Avril gasped, turning to Gideon, but for once he looked as out of control as she felt. He could not tear his eyes off Eddy and his jaw was hanging loose.

What looked like foam oozed a little way out of Eddy's mouth, and the juddering grew more intense. Her eyes were tight shut and her hair crackled outwards and upwards like a dark halo.

Then she slumped in the chair, and stopped moving.

'Edna!' Avril threw off Gideon's clutching, clawing fingers and lurched back to the chair. Then she let out a gasp.

The number on Eddy's left hand was gone.

'Edna, please . . .' Avril shook her. 'Gideon, what's happening? The number's gone, but she won't wake up!'

'Then it was too late,' Gideon rasped. His eyes were barely open now, and he could not lift his head. 'The cure came too late . . .' He tried to crawl an inch forward, but his body gave out. He lay still.

'She's in here!' came a yell as Augustus bowled into the lab, followed a second later by a gasping Wilfred. 'Have you saved her, Avril?' the dog shouted, running around in circles in his excitement.

'I thought I had.' Avril was still holding Eddy's limp left hand, too distraught to be surprised by Wilfred and Augustus' sudden appearance. 'But it was too late.'

'Too late?' Wilfred stared at her. 'It can't have been.'

'The number's gone,' Avril said, in despair, 'but she's not moving.'

'I don't believe you,' said Augustus. He leapt up on to Eddy's lap, shook his head violently to dislodge the last of the mud, and pressed an ear against Eddy's chest. His face was rigid for a moment. Then his tail twitched.

'Rubbish,' he said, rather shakily. 'She's not dead at all. I can hear her heart beating. Eddy! It's me, Gus! Eddy, you old faker!' He shook her by the arm with his teeth until her eyes opened.

Now they glowed as bright as ever.

'Eddy!' Wilfred rushed towards her, as Avril set about pulling the remaining shackle until it loosened, and eventually broke. 'I knew you'd make it!'

'Edna.' Avril put a trembling hand on the little girl's face. It felt warm to the touch again. 'You're all right. You're back.' She gulped in a very deep breath of air, pulled herself together, and reached for Eddy's hands. 'We have to get you out of here.'

'But . . . the Professor . . .' Eddy pointed towards the body on the floor. It had not moved, and did not appear to be breathing.

'I think it's too late,' Avril said. She slipped off her Santa cloak with shaking hands and placed it over Gideon's face. 'There was nothing we could do.'

Before anyone could speak, Augustus' ears snapped back. 'Bony!'

'Is he in trouble?'

'Sounds like it.' The dog was already bounding out of Lab 99. 'Hang on, Bony – I'm coming!'

'Us too!' Avril pulled Eddy and Wilfred towards the door, ushering them around Gideon's lifeless body. 'Don't look,' she begged them. 'We have to help Bony now.'

Eddy was at the top of the stairs, only a few steps behind Avril and Wilfred, when she stopped. 'Oh!' she said. 'Your fob watch, Avril. I'll catch you up in half a minute.' Eddy did not wait for Avril to disagree, and darted back towards Lab 99 as fast as she could run. There, she snatched up the fallen fob watch, then moved towards Gideon. Slowly, hardly daring to, she drew back the Santa cloak and looked down at Gideon's face. His eyes were tightly closed.

'Professor Blut,' she said.

There was no reply. Eddy took a step away, about to turn back to the door. Then Gideon spoke.

'Help me,' he said.

His eyes opened, and stared up into her own green eye. Eddy stood, rooted to the spot.

'How?' she asked, uncertainly.

'Find me some of that muffin.'

'I can't . . . I shouldn't . . .'

'You will,' Gideon said. His lips formed a smile. 'Because you are my flesh and blood.'

Eddy stared at him. She could not move for a moment. Then she found her voice. '*What did you say?*'

'You share my DNA.' Gideon's voice was weak and faint, but clear enough. 'I spilt a drop of my own blood into the mix that made you.'

Eddy's legs were shaking and her heart raced. She opened her mouth, but no words would come out. She could hardly believe what she was hearing. *Me – him – flesh and blood . . .*

'Don't you want to be like other children?' Gideon's voice was silky and gentle. 'Have a normal family?'

Eddy heard her voice before she even knew she had spoken. 'Yes . . . more than anything . . .'

'Then save me,' Gideon said, 'and I can make that happen.'

'What . . . what do you mean?'

'I could be your guardian,' said Gideon. 'Your *true* guardian, your kin. Not like Avril Crump. I could help you find your place in the real world. You won't have to hide away with that talking dog and that seven-foot freak.'

'Don't call them that!' Eddy clenched her fists. 'They're my friends . . .'

'Of course, of course. Forgive me. They are your friends.' Gideon spoke hastily. His green eyes were wide, suddenly the picture of sincerity. His frail left hand rose up, and took hold of Eddy's. 'But I am your father,' he said. '*Eddy.*'

'My father . . .'

Eddy's head was straining to take it all in. This was the man who, in the past, had tried to kill her friends, and experiment on her in the most horrible ways imaginable. But he was also her father. Almost in a dream, she walked to the leather chair, where a small pile of muffin morsels had gathered beneath an arm-rest. She jiggled them into her hand and walked back across the lab to where Gideon lay, his eyes closed again.

'Here,' she said, pouring the crumbs into his waiting mouth.

Gideon choked on the first few crumbs, then closed his mouth and swallowed.

Eddy watched, breathless, as he jolted once or twice, then lay very still. His blond hair began to fizz up around his head. With this halo of hair, and his pure, waxen skin, he looked almost like an angel. Then, after one final jolt, his eyes flew open.

They glowed a bright and beautiful green.

'Well,' he said. He sat up. 'It worked.'

Eddy took a stumbling step backwards, towards the door.

'Yes,' Gideon said, his voice silky smooth. 'You had better go.'

'But . . . about what you said . . . I love Avril . . .'

'Then for now, it is better that you go along with her. I will contact you when the time is right.'

Eddy nodded, gulped, and turned for the door.

'One more thing.' Gideon raised a hand. It was strong again. 'Keep our agreement to yourself. Can you do that for me?'

'Yes,' Eddy whispered. 'But . . . please, don't hurt my friends.'

'Oh, no. I shall do nothing of the sort.' Gideon bestowed a tender smile on her. 'Go now. But I will be in touch, Eddy. You can count on that.'

Eddy fled through the open door, not stopping to look back, and ran down the stairs as fast as she could.

She did not know that Wilfred had heard everything.

33

The Wisdom of Bonaparte

Bonaparte was white-faced. He clutched his three-cornered hat in front of him as if for protection, and looked from Lionel to O'Neill and back again with a growing expression of panic.

'Bony, listen to me . . .'

'No, Bony, listen to *me* . . .'

'I do not wish to listen to either of thee!' Bonaparte was close to tears. ''Twas my job to guard Bad Mr Lionel, and now I cannot even fulfil that simple task! What will they think of me? I have let Mr Dog down once more.'

'It's perfectly obvious. He's the one you're supposed to be guarding!' O'Neill jerked a thumb at his original. 'Now, come on, Bony . . .' O'Neill took an aggressive step towards Bonaparte and seized him by the right hand.

'This is stupid. You're coming with me.'

'No! He's coming with *me*!' Lionel grabbed Bonaparte's left hand.

O'Neill pulled. Lionel pulled harder.

'Oh! Take no offence – I am grateful for such ardent attention . . .' Bonaparte gasped, 'but 'tis a tad tough on my poor tendons . . .'

O'Neill dug his heels into the lino and pulled so hard that his hair stood on end, while Lionel gripped the floor with his toes and pulled so hard that his nose started to bleed.

'Let him go . . .'

'Let him go . . .'

'Let me go!' shrieked Bonaparte, as his shoulder sockets started to make alarming crunching sounds, and the pain in his elbows reached intolerable proportions.

Lionel suddenly glanced from the steely eyes of his clone to Bonaparte's contorted face, and came to his senses. 'What am I doing? I don't want to hurt you!' He let go his grip on Bonaparte's arm so fast that O'Neill flew backwards, taking Bonaparte with him.

'Bony, are you all right?' Lionel asked as O'Neill scrambled to his feet and began to help Bonaparte up.

'Of course he's all right. I won, didn't I?' said O'Neill. 'I'm your real friend, Bony, you see? I pulled harder.'

But Bonaparte did not budge. He wrapped his wounded arms about himself and stared down at O'Neill. 'Yes,' he said. 'And now I know who is my true friend.' Tears of pain and relief in his eyes, he walked towards Lionel. ''Tis thee,' he said, simply, putting his hand into Lionel's. 'I know that the real Mr Lionel would rather let me go with his clone than allow me to be torn in two.'

Lionel blinked at him. 'Bony. That's brilliant.'

'I did work it out all by myself,' Bonaparte said shyly. 'I think that now Mr Dog may forgive me for damaging his superpowers and destroying his beloved stick. For the first time, perhaps, Mr Dog may be proud of me.'

'Bony, I'm here!' Augustus appeared through the Tower doors at the end of the corridor, and hurtled towards them. 'What's happening? I heard you shouting.'

'All is well, dear Mr Dog.' Bonaparte said. 'I did

solve a Mr Lionel mystery, and now we know which is our true friend.'

'Bony was brilliant,' said Lionel, reaching up to pat the tall clone on the shoulder, then noticed that the corridor behind him was empty. 'He's gone! My clone's gone!'

'Lionel!' Avril came thudding from the other direction.

'Avril!' Lionel threw his arms around her middle. He tried to pick her up and swing her around, but common sense got the better of him. 'Where's Eddy?'

'She's all right, Lionel! We got there in time, and the muffin worked!' Avril picked Lionel up and spun him around with ease.

'Then where is she?'

'I'm here.' Eddy appeared through the Tower door and walked slowly towards them. Her face was pale, and she managed only a weak smile. 'I'm all right now.'

Behind her, coming through the Tower doors at an even slower pace, came Wilfred. His mind was reeling from what he had just seen and heard. *Professor Blut is Eddy's father?* As he approached the gathering in the middle of the corridor, he blinked frantically at Eddy, trying to get her attention without the others noticing.

'Eddy . . . *Eddy* . . .' But nobody heard him, least of all Eddy, as Bonaparte leapt at her with open arms.

'Miss Eddy! Hath yon terrible number disappeared from thy hand?'

'It's all gone, Bony.' Avril reached out a hand for Eddy's and squeezed it tightly. 'You're going to be all right, Edna!'

Eddy looked up at her. 'Yes. Everything's going to be all right.'

Wilfred stared at her. *All right?* What was she saying? 'But Eddy,' he blurted, 'Professor Blut . . .'

'Professor Blut is dead.' Eddy's eyes met Wilfred's for a moment, then she looked away.

'I wish we knew where that evil clone of me had gone,' said Lionel, recovered from his spin, and unable to tear his eyes off the beautiful Santa before him.

'We haven't got time to look for him,' Avril said. 'There are still security guards looking for us.'

Dr Wetherby let out a shriek to rival Bonaparte. 'Then we have to get out of here!'

'Chill out, Dad.' Wilfred sidled forward, trying one last time to catch Eddy's eye. His heart sank into his boots as she ignored him.

Dr Wetherby's eyes boggled, and his face turned

magenta. It was his turn to stammer. 'I beg your pardon?'

'He said chill out,' Augustus bounced happily into the fray, only to be interrupted by Wilfred.

'No, Augustus. I can handle this.' He looked up at Dr Wetherby again. 'I'm glad you're all right, Dad,' he said. 'I've got a lot of adventures to tell you about. If you'd like to hear them.'

Dr Wetherby's mouth hung open.

'We really ought to be getting out of here,' Avril said gently, pulling Eddy towards the lobby, and indicating that Lionel should follow. 'And then we've all got some stories to tell.'

Augustus' ears were drooping as he looked up at Bonaparte. 'The kid didn't need me,' he said sorrowfully. '*You* didn't need me.'

'Oh, Mr Dog!' Bonaparte scooped Augustus into his arms and began to trot after Avril, Eddy and Lionel. 'I shall always need thee! Why, who else am I to write my ballads about?'

'Any old hero would do,' sulked Augustus.

'Never!' Bonaparte laid a hand across his heart. 'There is no hero to touch thee, Mr Dog. No hero who is also such a dear friend.'

'Well . . .' Augustus' ears perked up, and his fur fizzed with pleasure. 'You're right there, Bony. I *am* rather marvellous on both counts. I think the occasion calls for a triumphal march, don't you?'

'And a triumphal stew!' cried Bonaparte.

'A triumphal pizza,' said Augustus, 'will do.' He looked up at Bonaparte. 'You can have some,' he added carelessly, 'if you want. You've had a bit of a triumph too.'

'Oh, Mr Dog! And already, the first lines of my latest triumphal ode are beginning to take shape . . .'

Behind the humming tall clone, Dr Wetherby and Wilfred walked alongside each other in silence. Wilfred could not stop thinking about what Eddy had just said: '*Professor Blut is dead.*' The words had tripped so easily out of his friend's mouth. *She lied to me*, he thought, sharp tears pricking at the back of his eyes. *Eddy lied to me.*

Then Dr Wetherby spoke. 'Wilfred, are you all right?'

'Fine, Dad.'

'I'd . . . like to hear your stories,' Dr Wetherby continued, stiffly. 'You've had quite a day, haven't you,' – he swallowed – 'son?'

Wilfred pushed his glasses up his nose and looked up at his father. 'You too, Dad,' he said. He tried to tear his mind off Eddy's disturbing behaviour. But it was not simply her lie that was troubling him. If what Gideon had said was true . . .

'Perhaps we can have a hot chocolate,' suggested Dr Wetherby, as purple as he had ever been, 'and . . . rent a DVD from the shop, and . . . er . . . talk?'

Wilfred's jaw dropped slightly, and he stared up at his father. This was the second most surprising thing he had heard all day. 'I'd really like that.' He smiled shyly up at his father. 'Unless there's a documentary you'd like to watch?'

'No. I'd like something fun to watch after losing my job.'

On an ordinary day, this would have been an enormous shock to Wilfred, but now he simply reached for Dr Wetherby's hand in wordless understanding. He knew exactly how his father felt. He had lost his job. And Wilfred had lost his best friend.

'You don't have to tell me about that now,' he said, and saw the relief flood across his father's face. 'Let's just go home.'

Bruised and battered, her usually sleek dark hair wild and her long red nails broken, Sedukta staggered towards the back entrance. She propped the wrecked motorbike up against the wall, and was about to use her skeleton key when the radio in her pocket buzzed.

'Sedukta . . .' came Gideon's voice, strong and clear. 'Sedukta, are you there?'

Sedukta scrabbled for the radio. 'Yes, Professor . . . but things did not go to plan. The bike crashed . . . the Crump woman got away – it was all the guards' fault – I have dealt with them . . .'

'The guards are dealt with? Excellent. That was just what I was about to tell you to do.'

Sedukta gasped with relief. 'Oh, Professor . . .'

'Deal with O'Neill too. He has no use in my new plans. Find him and eliminate him.'

'Of course, Professor. But the Crump woman . . .'

'Never mind her – for now. Just come to Lab 99 when you have completed your assignment. We have work to do.'

There was a pause on the line, and then Gideon's voice rang out again, clearer than ever.

'*I'm going to get my daughter back.*'

★

The huge iron gates were swinging open as the party walked slowly across the car park. 'Well done, Lionel!' Avril called, as he came racing out of the oak door from the Control Centre. 'Now we can get out of here once and for all! I never want to come back to Leviticus again.'

'Hurry up, Crumpy!' Augustus was already inside the Mini, happily sitting in the driver's seat and sounding the horn with his nose, while Bonaparte scribbled down his latest triumphal ode. 'It's triumphal pizza time! Last one home gets all the olives.'

'Thank you, Avril.' Eddy held Avril back for a moment. 'Thank you for saving me.'

'Glad to,' blushed Avril. 'Never been gladder.' She stroked Eddy's hair for a moment, then said the words she had wanted to say for hours. 'Let's go home.'

'Yes,' said Eddy. She turned and stared up at the West Tower, before following Avril out of the tall gates. 'Home.'

'Quiet, everyone!' came Augustus' voice again. 'Bony's got my triumphal ode all ready . . .'

And as the yellow Mini pulled away from Leviticus Laboratories, Bonaparte began to sing.

TO BE CONTINUED . . .

Heroic Mr Dog – the Bottom Biter

A hero such as Hercules doth get a faultless press.
How the Hydra multiplied its
heads is anybody's guess.
Though H's heart was filled with dread,
he kept his (solitary) head,
and burnt yon Hydra til it bred
significantly less.
Now, if Mr Dog went head-to-head
with beasts from Ancient Greece
(on his way from wooing sirens
and bedecked in Golden Fleece),
then to make the mythic monster slump,
our Mr Dog would simply jump

and bite that Hydra's writhing rump
and thus restore the peace!
CHORUS

His many talents do abound.
His paws stay firmly on the ground.
A braver hound
Could ne'er be found
Than wondrous Mr Dog!

The great and noble Arthur
faced a challenge of his own:
'twas to excavate Excalibur
with naught but strength from stone.
Achieving this, the king was able
to seat around his sturdy table
a dozen knights – so goes yon fable –
and never fought alone.
Compare with this, I beg thee,
Mr Dog's impressive feat.
For he never hollers 'Help!'
when there are villains to be beat.
He needeth not a noble knight
to back him up while he doth fight!
His legendary bottom-bite

is swift and sharp and sweet.

CHORUS

His many talents do abound.
His paws stay firmly on the ground.
A finer hound
Could ne'er be found
Than splendid Mr Dog!

A man named Alexander
led his armies 'cross the East.
He marched through day
and marched through night
til several were deceased.
But was it not a nasty mission
to conquer all the competition
without the thought to ask permission?
Why – at the very least!
Now, Mr Dog might conquer,
but he adds a pretty please.
And Mr Dog doth win his fights,
but wins his fights with ease.
Behold that sleek and honed exterior!
Our hero's style is so superior:
a nip upon his foe's posterior

doth bring them to their knees.

CHORUS

His many talents do abound.

His paws stay firmly on the ground.

A nicer hound

Could ne'er be found

Than fame-eschewing, trouser-chewing,

baddie-fighting, bottom-biting,

caring, sharing, daring Mr Dog!

'Angela Woolfe has created a winning formula, combining comic characters, true friendship and a pacy plot with, at times, a very real sense of menace. More please!'

Philip Ardagh